A CAT IN
THE WINGS

A Cat in the Wings

An Alice Nestleton Mystery

Lydia Adamson

Thorndike Press • Chivers Press
Waterville, Maine USA   Bath, England

This Large Print edition is published by Thorndike Press, USA and by Chivers Press, England.

Published in 2001 in the U.S. by arrangement with NAL Signet, a division of Penguin Putnam Inc.

Published in 2001 in the U.K. by arrangement with NAL Signet, a division of Penguin Putnam Inc.

U.S. Hardcover 0-7862-3676-0 (Mystery Series Edition)
U.K. Hardcover 0-7540-4726-1 (Chivers Large Print)

The first chapter of this book previously appeared in *A Cat by Any Other Name*.

The text of this Large Print edition is unabridged.
Other aspects of the book may vary from the original edition.

Set in 16 pt. Plantin by Al Chase.

Printed in the United States on permanent paper.

British Library Cataloguing-in-Publication Data available

Library of Congress Cataloging-in-Publication Data

Adamson, Lydia.
    A cat in the wings : an Alice Nestleton mystery /
by Lydia Adamson.
    p.   cm.
    ISBN 0-7862-3676-0 (lg. print : hc : alk. paper)
    1. Nestleton, Alice (Fictitious character) — Fiction.
2. Women detectives — New York (State) — New York —
Fiction.   3. Women cat owners — Fiction.   4. New York
(N.Y.) — Fiction.   5. Ballet dancers — Fiction.   6. Cats —
Fiction.   7. Large type books.   I. Title.
PS3551.D3954 C383 2001
813'.54—dc21   2001053014

A Cat in
the Wings

1

Think of the music and costumes and excitement of *The Nutcracker*!

As performed on Christmas Eve by the New York City Ballet at Lincoln Center.

Is there any other event that so captures the desperate holiday gaiety of Manhattan?

I doubt it.

But what was I doing there, in a first-tier box, with five kiddies?

Yes, count 'em. Five. Between the ages of six and ten.

There was Kathy, Laura, Stephen, Edward. And one whose name may have been "Ada" or "Dada" or "Sadie."

I was there because, in a moment of hubris, I had bragged to one of my cat-sitting clients that I could get good tickets to *The Nutcracker* anytime I wanted.

Mrs. Timmerman was wide-eyed when I announced that. She asked: "But how?"

"A friend in high places," I replied mysteriously.

Indeed, I did have a friend in a high place. Lucia Maury worked in the executive offices of the Lincoln Center for the Performing Arts. Her responsibilities included making travel arrangements for the New York City Ballet when the troupe went on tour. I had known Lucia for more than twenty years. We had been roommates when we both arrived in Manhattan — she to dance, and I to act. We had kept in touch, one reason being that we shared a passion for Maine coon cats. Lucia had once had a wonderful Maine coon named Splat, who passed away about three years ago. She was so distraught that she never obtained another cat. Lucia was a very fine dancer until she hurt her knee. After joining Lincoln Center in an administrative capacity, she had always offered me tickets, most of which I had refused.

The only flaw in our relationship was that I was profoundly jealous of her — while she was dancing. Like many actresses, I have this inferiority complex in relation to ballet dancers. They are so bloody wonderful! They do what we yearn to do and never can.

Anyone who has been backstage just before a ballet starts knows what I mean. The dancers are chatting about everything from boyfriends to shopping trips to the weather. Some are stretching. Some are putting on their makeup.

Suddenly the orchestra begins, and a few

seconds later the curtain goes up.

One of the dancers, who moments earlier was chewing on a fingernail because she was bored, bursts out onto the stage and executes a series of magnificent leaps and turns.

She stops suddenly downstage, bows luxuriously, and then proceeds to glissade contemptuously about the stage.

In a short span of time the dancer has gone from quiescence to ecstasy, with many stops in between — a disciplined orgy of physical elegance and control.

How could an actress *not* be jealous of a ballerina?

But, to make a long story short, Mrs. Timmerman, that day, was annoying me. She kept going on and on about her country house in Dutchess County, and how this Christmas they had decided to stay in Manhattan to let the children experience "an urban Christmas." And besides, the cat Belle hated the country.

On and on she went, and I had to listen politely. The more she talked the more she irritated me. So I just casually mentioned that I could get any kind of ballet tickets, including ones for *The Nutcracker* on Christmas Eve. It was my way of showing her that while I might be a cat-sitter, I had another life — a life that was far superior to hers, culturally, no matter what her wealth.

It was kind of pathetic. I didn't usually do those kinds of petty things. But Christmas in New York is difficult, even if one is a Minnesota farm girl who has lived in Manhattan for more than two decades. And the conversation with Mrs. Timmerman took place only nineteen days before Christmas.

Compounding my stupidity, I offered to take the children as well as obtain the tickets. Everyone was ecstatic except for the cat, Belle, and me.

So that is why, on Christmas Eve, I found myself shepherding the kiddies at *The Nutcracker*. That is why I had ended up sitting in an opulent box seat at the State Theater, amidst all that Noel splendor of light and color and music and fantasy.

Actually, Tchaikovsky has always been too much for me, so after the first dazzling scene I let my mind wander back in time, as I tried to envision what the first production of *Nutcracker* in America must have looked like. It took place in 1940, before I was born, at the old Metropolitan Opera House. The company was the Ballet Russe de Monte Carlo. The sugar-plum fairy was Alicia Markova. The prince was André Eglevsky.

When my efforts to conjure up the scene failed, I just let myself doze off, since my charges were mesmerized by the balletic spectacle.

My doze turned into a gentle fantasy in which my two cats, Bushy and Pancho, were in the process of trying out for roles in an all-feline production of *The Nutcracker*.

I opened my eyes just as, onstage, the Mouse King was about to be extirpated by the heroine.

The door to our box had been pushed open a few inches.

Lucia Maury was standing there. I hadn't even known she would be at the performance. She hadn't mentioned it.

She didn't move. She held a finger up to her lips, as if to signify that the children shouldn't know she was there. It was very odd.

Then she waved one hand, indicating that I should leave the box.

I did so. The children were too caught up in the ballet to even notice my departure.

The moment I had stepped outside the box and closed the door gently behind me, I knew Lucia was in some kind of trouble. Her thin, angular body was stooped over. She was very pale. The long sleeves of her lovely black dress were pulled up to her elbows, as if she were about to do manual labor.

"Lucia! What's the matter?"

She started to answer, then burst into tears. She fought back the tears, grabbed my arm, and started to pull me along.

I allowed myself to be led. Lounging ushers stared at us. The music from within could be heard only faintly.

She guided me through the mezzanine lobby, past the bar, already set up for the coming intermission, and through the glass doors onto the open-air balcony.

It was cold. A strong wind was blowing. The city was a bonfire of holiday lights. The fountain in the plaza below was spouting magnificently. I could hear the bells of the Salvation Army Santas on Broadway.

At first I thought we were the only ones on that windswept balcony.

But then I saw a small knot of people on the western edge, against the building. At least two of them were police officers.

Lucia was beginning to shiver. She had stopped about five feet from the gathering.

Suddenly I knew why we were there.

Sitting up against the building wall was a derelict, without shoes.

His eyes, a startling shade of blue, were wide open.

I was about to remonstrate with Lucia for having dragged me out onto a freezing balcony to look at a drunk. After all, there were hundreds of derelicts like this one living around Lincoln Center.

But then I noticed something else distinctive about this drunk — something other than his beautiful eyes and the fact that he was shoeless in December.

There was a hole in his forehead. A small, jagged hole.

The man was dead. And the hole had been made by a bullet.

Lucia increased the pressure of her arm on mine, as if she were falling.

"It's Dobrynin, Alice," she said. "Dobrynin!"

Was Lucia mad?

"Do you mean *Peter* Dobrynin?"

"Yes! Yes! Yes!" she whispered frantically. "It's Peter!" And her fingers pinched my arm so forcefully that I cried out from the pain. One of the policemen turned to stare at me.

Peter Dobrynin? I stared at the shoeless dead man again. How could it be?

Peter Dobrynin had dropped out of the public eye three years ago. The most acclaimed male ballet dancer since Nijinsky had gone into seclusion. There were all kinds of rumors and speculations: He had gone into a drug-rehab clinic. He had entered a monastery in Vermont. He had been admitted to a mental hospital. No one knew the real story.

But what an impact this one-time student at the Kirov had made on the dance world before he dropped out! Bigger and more powerful and dramatic than Baryshnikov . . . more technically proficient and more musical than Nureyev . . . his roles in *Giselle* and *Firebird* and *Petrouchka* had made him the new hero of the American ballet.

And Dobrynin had been as flamboyant offstage as he was on — lover, brawler, lunatic, junkie, drunk, frequenter of jet-set parties as well as trend-setting Harlem clubs. He was always out of control.

Lucia started to pull me away, but I resisted. I couldn't stop looking at the corpse.

Had this wreck of a man really once been the golden dancer Dobrynin?

The wind began to whip across the open expanse of concrete, making me shudder. After all, it was Christmastime in the city.

2

Lucia spent the night on my sofa. But even after two cups of hot tea, lemon, and brandy, she wasn't able to sleep much.

I could hear her pacing and crying, so around two in the morning I carried my bedding into the living room and stayed with her there. The floor was hard, and my Maine coon cat Bushy refused to leave the bedroom pillow to keep me company on the vigil. So much for feline constancy.

Pancho, the other cat, who seemed never to sleep more than forty seconds at a time, did stop briefly to sniff me several times during his perpetual flight from imagined enemies. I was thankful for that.

Finally, around four, Lucia fell into a heavy sleep.

At nine in the morning she was still sleeping soundly, so I went down to buy the newspaper and croissants. It was Christmas Day, and some sort of treat seemed in order.

The early-morning streets were very still — not a creature was stirring, as the poem would have it. But, to my relief, the French bakery was open. I used the change in my

15

pocket to buy a *Daily News* from one of those blasted automated boxes, losing only a dime in the transaction.

I heard Lucia stir while I was making the coffee.

"I'm sorry I was such a baby last night, Alice. It was all too much for me. And now here I am ruining your holiday."

She stood just outside my small kitchen. It was amazing how little her firm dancer's body had aged. And her high-cheekboned face was still thin as well, her features crisp. Lucia's mid-length sandy hair was pulled back into a ponytail. She looked as though she were about to do a barre.

"It's good to have you here, no matter what the circumstances," I said. We used to stay over at each other's place a lot in the old days. "And besides, you know I've been a bah-humbug type about Christmas for ages. Remember?"

She nodded quietly and helped me bring the coffee and croissants out to the living room. Bushy, having finally made his first regal appearance of the morning, was now inspecting Lucia minutely, probably calculating how long it was going to take to make her his slave.

We read the *News* article together, when we finally managed to find it. The first two

16

pages of the Christmas Day edition were filled with peace-on-earth stories and Santas and happy families; Bethlehem guarded by heavily armed Israeli soldiers; stock photos of St. Patrick's Cathedral during midnight Mass; crêche scenes from the outer boroughs. Peter Dobrynin's death had been pushed all the way back to page five.

A DANCER DIES, the bold headline read.

There were several photos of Dobrynin as he had appeared in his choicest roles. And there was a single grainy, grim shot of the hospital stretcher carrying the covered body to a waiting ambulance.

Alongside the photographs, a few paragraphs of text in a box traced for one last time Peter Dobrynin's meteoric rise in the ballet world — and his equally meteoric fall.

The story was short and to the point:

Acclaimed ballet dancer Peter Dobrynin was found shot to death in the State Theater at Lincoln Center last night, during the New York City Ballet's traditional Christmas Eve performance of Tchaikovsky's *Nutcracker.* The dead Dobrynin was shoeless.

Lincoln Center staffers first believed the dead man to be a neighborhood derelict who had managed to enter the theater unnoticed. But several balletgoers noticed the similarity between him and Dobrynin, who has been out of the public eye in recent years. A positive identification was made later.

Police say they know of no motive for the killing at this time. There are no suspects, and no actual witnesses to the crime. The murder weapon has not been recovered. According to authorities, Dobrynin was most likely shot on the theater's outdoor balcony during the opening scenes of the ballet.

End of story. Obviously, the murder had occurred too late in the evening for the reporter to garner the usual eulogies. The remainder of the paper's holiday edition seemed to be taken up with stories about luckless policemen and other vital city workers who had to work on Christmas Day.

Lucia pushed the paper away, toward the center of the table. We looked at each other. What was there to say, "Merry Christmas"? She took a sip of her coffee.

"No Christmas tree, Alice?" she said, looking around.

I laughed a little. It's true, I had placed a

wreath on my front door, but that was only because the makers of a hand lotion, for whom I had done some voice-overs, had sent it to me. It had looked just too green and beautiful to throw away.

"I haven't had a tree in years," Lucia admitted. Then she smiled. "Have you ever noticed what sad creatures Christmas trees are?"

I knew she was talking about something else, not trees, but I didn't know how to respond.

Lucia took her coffee cup and wandered over to the window with it. I stayed where I was and left her to her thoughts.

After a few moments, I saw her tense as she peered down at the street.

"Oh, look!" she exclaimed.

"What is it?" I started to rise.

"Oh . . . No, nothing. I thought I saw a group of children caroling."

"Not in *this* neighborhood, dear," I said. I was preparing to make a cynical remark as to the only reason I could think of for a group of youngsters to be congregating in my neighborhood. But Lucia had turned away from the window by then, and I saw the anguish on her face.

"Horrible, horrible!" she wailed, her face in her hands. "Damn horrible Christmas!"

19

As I sat watching my distraught friend crying her eyes out, I had a sudden and anomalous memory of one of the many happy Christmas celebrations I had had with my grandmother in Minnesota. Christmas at home on the farm had had no religious overtones whatever, but it was always special — everything about it. The graceful untrimmed spruce that dwarfed the enclosed porch; the chores that had to be done whether it was Christmas or not; the enormous breakfast of pancakes and preserves and delicious sausages made by a neighbor and presented to Gram; the functional gifts — mostly clothes, and almost always winter clothes; and finally, the money Gram would always give me in a plain envelope — "to spend on any wicked thing you please," she would say happily.

But now, I had no choice but to turn back to the unhappy woman weeping in front of my living room window. I went to her and put my arms around her, leading her back to her seat.

"I had to . . . identify . . . him, Alice! Can you imagine what it was like? He was so . . . so . . . his eyes, staring, wide-open like that! And that terrible hole in his head! You just don't know what it was like!"

I thought it best not to interrupt Lucia to

say that I certainly did know. I'd had my own brushes with violent death.

"I want to tell you something, Alice." She was a little calmer now, taking a few sips of coffee. "It's something . . . very private."

I waited.

"About four years ago, I had — Dobrynin and I were lovers for a time."

My incredulity must have shown quite baldly.

"Yes," Lucia went on, as if addressing my disbelief. "I had an affair with him."

Decorous, proper Lucia — like me, a middle-aged woman — and the maniacal seducer Dobrynin? I suppose I've heard more preposterous confessions, but at that moment none came to mind. It seemed crazy. Like the Queen of England confiding that she'd had an affair with Fidel Castro. Or Dietrich Fischer-Dieskau revealing he'd been the longtime lover of Janis Joplin.

Lucia Maury was and always had been a sweet person. She had come to New York from Delaware. Her family was wealthy and strait-laced in equal measure — which is to say, very much so. In fact, they were out-and-out puritans. And so, in her way, was Lucia, despite her cultural sophistication and experience. Even in what was supposed to have been her "wild" twenties, I had never seen her take a drink or smoke a cigarette. In fact I'd never seen her do so much as stay up past midnight. She was all hard work and discipline and veneration of the arts.

And now she was telling me that she'd had an affair with a satyr. A great dancer, yes. But a wild man — especially in the sexual arena. Dobrynin's promiscuity and inventiveness were legendary. Apparently he had delighted in providing endless grist for the tabloids and the gossip columns.

"I loved him very much, Alice," she whispered. "We loved each other, I mean."

Of course I didn't say so, but I doubted that. Dobrynin probably loved ballet and booze and himself, I thought, and almost certainly not in that order.

"He was not what people said he was." Lucia was on her feet again. "Believe me, Alice. Peter was kind and beautiful. . . ." She paused and turned back toward the window before continuing. "It's just so terrible, so sad. He could have been the greatest dancer who ever lived."

She reached down and grasped my hand then. "Say you'll come with me to the funeral. Please, Alice."

"Of course, Lucia. If that's what you

want. But for now, why don't you sit down and relax?"

She shook her head. "No. I have to be going now."

"Then let me take you home," I suggested.

"No," she said firmly. "You've done enough. Bless you, Alice." And with that, she gathered her things and left.

3

I stepped inside the cavernous Russian Orthodox church with Lucia, and knew immediately that we were in a strange land. There were flowers everywhere, and incense and brilliantly brocaded priestly garments. This, I could tell, would be the kind of funeral an irreverent actor friend of mine has dubbed "a smells-and-bells show."

The mourners were no less elegant, ornate, and magisterial. Everywhere you looked was rich black velvet, fur, flowing chiffon; pale, flawless skin, swathed in somber finery.

In stark contrast to all this was the coffin, which was plain and closed and utterly free of ornamentation.

Lucia and I sat in a rear pew and watched the proceedings unfold. These ballet people provided quite the spectacle. They moved noiselessly, regally up and down the aisles, as if they were on a promenade in some other century. Young and old, famous or infamous or simply unknown, they all seemed to share a stylized appearance that was almost absurd in its theatricality.

Lucia leaned into me conspiratorially. "There's Louis Beasley," she whispered, nodding toward a portly man taking his seat several rows ahead of us. "And that's Vol with him."

Beasley, the impresario who had "discovered" Dobrynin, had the look of a well-fed kitchen cat. He was decked out in a long beaver coat. His younger lover, Vol Teak, looked more the feral Siamese. The two had entered the church and strode up the aisle as if they were about to go out onto the balcony of their Venice hotel room to take the sun.

"Look!" Lucia whispered again, urgently this time. "There's Melissa!"

I turned my head obliquely and saw ex-ballerina Melissa Taniment seating herself alongside her husband. She was still graceful, striking, with those hypnotizing hazel eyes. Dobrynin had been catapulted to fame when Melissa chose him to partner her in *Giselle*. Their subsequent affair had been intense, stormy, and a staple of the gossip-and-society pages.

Then Lucia pointed out in quick succession: Betty Ann Ellenville, the ballet critic whose articles had helped create Dobrynin's reputation; Maggie Brown, one of Dobrynin's teachers; Dr. James Broga, the dancer's physician, a specialist in dance-related injuries; and half a dozen others. Lucia was a veritable tour guide to the world of ballet society, but her monologue was interrupted by the first wail of the chanting priests.

At the conclusion of the service, Louis Beasley walked briskly up to the pulpit for the eulogy. His voice was a commanding, if affected, one.

"This!" He gestured toward the plain coffin. "This is what awaits all the young gods. Madness and death. Death and madness. Nijinsky went mad. And so, finally, did Dobrynin." Beasley paused a minute. "Peter Dobrynin was what every dancer yearns to be. Guileless. Without affectation. Purity of line. Purity of soul.

"But it is as La Rochefoucauld said: 'Death and the sun cannot be looked at steadily.' And so, when we remember Dobrynin, it will not be his horrible death, the loss of his brilliance, that we recall. No, we will remember only Dobrynin dancing."

Here, Beasley grasped at the ends of his long red cashmere muffler. He paced for a moment.

From the pews, for the first time, came the sounds of weeping. I wanted to look around, to locate the person doing the

26

crying, but it seemed scandalously inappropriate, so I kept my eyes on Beasley.

"What do I remember of Peter Dobrynin? I will tell you." And here he paused momentarily, swallowing audibly. "I remember the beginning of the coda of the Black Swan pas de deux. I remember Peter as Siegfried — his series of grand jetés. I remember that as I watched him dance I was filled with a beauty and strength and wisdom that only he could evoke."

Now the tears cascaded down the impresario's cheeks and threatened to choke him. His last words were unclear. I think he said something fairly standard, like "Good-bye, dear Dobrynin. Rest well."

There was such a lost look in Lucia's eyes. "I never saw him do the Black Swan pas de deux," she confided in a whisper, sounding utterly crushed.

Beasley's lover was assisting him from the pulpit. The lights illuminated Vol Teak's profile just then, and I realized he was not as young as his manner of dressing suggested.

"Look at Melissa!" Lucia urged. "Look at her face!"

I turned to look at the beautiful ballerina, now retired for more than five years. What I saw startled me. Her lovely face was deathly still — not a flicker of an expression on it. She might have been in a trance, or listening to something no one else could hear.

I felt Lucia tremble beside me, sensed that she was beginning to fall apart again. I placed my hand in hers and she met my eyes and nodded once, thankfully.

Then, what I found myself hoping would be the final procession began. First came the priests, chanting and swinging the censers. Slowly they left the church, followed by the pallbearers and the coffin, and then the mourners.

"I don't want to go to the cemetery. I just don't!"

I turned to reassure the obviously shaken Lucia, who had forgotten that we had decided beforehand not even to try to get out to the cemetery. We were by no means close relations of the deceased, so there would be no room for us in the limousines — and neither of us had a car.

The two of us had just stepped out of the church when the person in front of me — it was the writer Betty Ann Ellenville — stopped abruptly.

I banged into her, sending her off-balance and setting off a chain reaction of stumbling and startled cries.

I suddenly noticed, however, that *all* the

mourners seemed to be tripping over one another.

"What is going *on?*" Lucia hissed.

I could see that the forward motion of the coffin had ceased before it reached the street. Now everyone was crying out and pointing. There was a growing, palpable sense of danger.

I pulled Lucia toward the door at the side of the church. We would have more room there and would be able to see the street — and locate the source of the bottleneck.

The procession had halted on the steps because the hearse was not ready to receive the coffin.

On the side of the hearse facing the church, someone had painted graffiti in large, blood-red letters. It must have been done while the drawn-out ceremony was in progress, with the drivers no doubt off somewhere having coffee.

Now all the drivers were using gloves, caps, pieces of paper, anything they could find, in a frantic attempt to wipe away the words.

The words on the car read: ANNA PAVLOVA SMITH.

Nothing more.

Everyone knew who Anna Pavlova was. But who on earth was Anna Pavlova *Smith?*

Lucia didn't know. Nor did I. Nor did anyone else in the crowd. The consensus was that the funeral had been infiltrated by one of that army of deranged celebrity-worshipers — or celebrity-bashers — who stalk events such as this one.

The men could not remove the scrawled red letters. They gave up and loaded the hearse. Finally all the cars took off. Peter Dobrynin was to be buried in his mother's family plot in Connecticut.

I walked Lucia to Park Avenue and saw her into a taxi. Then I headed downtown, walking into the bright winter wind. For everyone else on the street, perhaps this was just a pleasant post-Christmas afternoon. But I felt oddly oppressed by it. The sun was out, and I was all bundled up . . . yet I felt myself slowly turning numb.

4

About thirty-six hours before the dawn of the
new year, Tony Basillio came rapping on my
door. It was his usual mode of arrival — completely unannounced. Out-of-the-blue
Basillio.

Tony was exhibiting that brand of propri-
etary behavior typical of the ex-lover, but
from the looks of him now was no time for
me to carp: He appeared to be crazier than
ever. It was apparent that his plunge back
into the world of the theater — after more
than a decade of being a good citizen — was
taking him deeper and deeper into murky
waters.

"Well, Swede," he announced broadly,
"here I am at last. I know how madly you've
missed me. I could tell by all those desperate, pleading letters and phone calls of
yours."

"Don't you chastise me, Tony. I didn't
even know where you were living the last
few months."

He scooped into his arms the preening
Bushy and collapsed along with the cat onto
the sofa.

"I could use a brandy, Swede," he said wearily. "Or in lieu of that, you could bring me an order of rye toast with a schmeer of scallion cream cheese."

"I don't have any scallion cream cheese, and you know it."

"Then a brandy it is, my girl."

He grinned as I delivered the drink.

"You're more beautiful than ever, Swede," he said. "Can we make love now — right this instant?"

I ignored the question. Bushy seized the opportunity to escape from Tony's grasp.

"What are you up to, Tony?" I asked, a little suspicious.

He gave me the killer smile again, only this time he shivered, too. As usual, he was underdressed. I saw then that his distinguished, pockmarked face was red from the cold. He had grown his hair quite long, and it was all over the place. Well, I thought, at least he hasn't succumbed to the Middle-Aged Man with Ponytail Syndrome. In fact, it's hard to believe he *is* a middle-aged man.

"Swede," he replied languorously, using that silly name for me that he alone used, "I'm up to no good — and loving it."

Tony stretched luxuriously.

No, the name "Swede" had no relation whatever to the reality of my life. For while I am indeed tall and fair, I in no way look like a Swede, nor am I one.

"I spend my time," he was saying, "going from party to fabulous party. Attracting beautiful young actresses. And when I spot one about nineteen, just in from the provinces, with that long golden hair and that firm, ripe body and that hungry look on her face . . . why, then I just tell her who I am.

"And of course she's never heard of me. So I tell her that I'm such a famous designer that Olivier himself, in the old days, would never contract to appear in an American production unless he knew I was doing the sets.

"Then I invite her up to my room to look at my . . . uh . . . *sketches* for the Theban Cycle sets. And then I promise to make her a star and she melts in my arms. You know the drill, Miss Nestleton.

"So there you have it. That's what I've been up to."

He held out his empty glass for a refill.

"Oh, right, Tony," I said, not taking it from his fingers. "Meanwhile, back in your real life, what are you up to?"

"Get me another brandy first, Swede."

"I don't know, Tony. The bottle's pretty near empty."

"But it's the holidays!"

Feigning reluctance, I took the glass and refilled it.

"The truth is, I *have* been to a couple of parties lately. In fact, at one of those Christmas Eve do's your name was mentioned prominently."

"My name? Who by?"

"Some producer. I don't remember his name."

Against my will, "What did he say?" came out.

Tony laughed, and took a slow sip of his brandy before proceeding. He was purposely being difficult.

"The man said, and I quote, 'Alice Nestleton is one of the best actresses out there today, but she'll never be rich and famous . . . never be a star . . . never arrive at a restaurant in a limo . . . she'll never have a summer place on Dune Road.' "

"He forgot, 'Never be able to hire a tailor to let out her camel-hair coat.' Come on, Tony. You're making this up."

"I'm not, Swede. I swear. I swear on your sainted grandmother's head. The guy said there were two reasons you never made it in the past — and won't make it in the future. First, he says, you're too old. Though I don't agree with that, babe. That was downright cruel. And second, says he, you're too goddamn stubborn — 'willful,' he called you. Willful. He said you always act like you're some kind of theatrical pope delivering holy instructions."

"Ha! And what did you say?"

"Me? Nothing. I wasn't a part of the conversation. I was merely eavesdropping."

"Um-hum." I nodded. "And you can't remember his name."

"Nope. But he said you were up for one of his shows and you didn't get it. It was something called *The Interesting Mrs. Heath* or something like that. He said you didn't get it because you refused to use the proper accent. The part was an upper-class California WASP. And you told the director that California WASPs sound like Memphis hookers and you don't do Southern accents. Or something like that."

"What nonsense!" I exploded. "Of *course* I read for that part. About seven months ago. The name of the play was *The Interrogation of Mrs. Heath*. 'Interrogation,' Tony, not 'interesting.' And I wasn't 'up' for anything. I *had* the part!

"Plus — I did *not* argue with the director about any phony accent. The argument was about his using an overhead movie screen for some ungodly, *arty* commentary during the performance. It was one of the most hid-

35

eously fake modern props that ever saw the light of day — just intolerably cute. And I'd rather earn my daily bread worming foul-tempered cats for the rest of my life than deal with a fool director who doesn't know his —"

"Swede," Tony broke in, interrupting my harangue, "it's all, as they say, blood under the bridge. I'm just reporting what I heard. What else am I good for these days?"

"You seem to be doing well enough seducing those young things."

"They do go for me, it's true. I guess it's my European soul — I'm right out of the Renaissance, you know. That, and my obvious desperation."

I had been holding Bushy, reassuring him after his brief imprisonment by Tony, who now stood up and took the cat gently from my arms and placed him on the floor.

"Why'd you do that?"

"I don't think I trust that guy."

"Who, Bushy? He's the best friend I ever had," I said. "You know me, Tony: Love me, love my cat."

"Okay."

He gave me a rather long kiss which I didn't interrupt.

Bushy growled.

"Listen," said Tony confidentially, the

brandy obviously beginning to work on him. "I think we have to use the Henry Wyatt test to judge that cat's character."

"Henry who?"

"Sir Henry Wyatt," he said, "was thrown into a dungeon by Richard the Third for his Lancastrian sympathies. You remember the War of the Roses, don't you?"

"Tony, what does this have to do with Bushy?"

"Well, dungeons in those days were no joke. And the only reason old Sir Henry survived was because of a small, sad-looking cat, who kept bringing him pigeons to eat. Now I ask you, Swede" — he looked down at Bushy — "would this beast do that for you? Could he pull it off?"

I didn't know how to answer that one. It was too bizarre a hypothetical. All I said was, "No more brandy, Tony."

"Good point," he agreed. "No more brandy. Let's do something else, Swede."

It was only the sudden ringing of the phone that threw Basillio off his game. Startled, he released me, and I picked it up before the second ring.

On the other end of the line was Lucia Maury. Her voice told me she was caught somewhere between paralysis and hysteria.

Her words came out in spastic bursts.

"Alice! The police are here — here in my apartment. Oh, Alice!" she wailed. "They think I . . . killed . . . Dobrynin."

"Tell me what happened, Lucia. Try to stay calm."

But she couldn't. I could barely make out her words. She was screeching something about a search warrant. "Help me!" was all I could understand unequivocally.

"I'm on the way, Lucia — all right? I'll be there in ten minutes — all right?"

The phone went dead. I looked around for Tony, who was on all fours, dangling a toy mouse in front of a wary Bushy.

"Tony, I've got to go. Stay here if you want. I'll tell you about it later. Play with the cats!"

I grabbed my bag and my parka and slammed the door behind me. Halfway down the stairs I realized I'd forgotten my gloves. I didn't go back.

5

Lucia lived in a massive old apartment building on Fifty-seventh Street between Eighth and Ninth avenues. And a rare building it was, featuring sprawling apartments, immaculately kept lobby and corridors, flawless building services, ancient uniformed doormen — in other words, all the longed-for and welcomed civilities. And it was rent-stabilized! I, along with millions of others, would cheerfully have killed for one of those apartments.

The apartment door was ajar when I arrived. As soon as I stepped inside I was struck by the bustle of activity. Uniformed and plainclothes officers were rustling back and forth. But a rigid and wide-eyed Lucia sat silently in the center of the living room on a plain wooden chair.

I walked quickly toward her.

"Who are you?" A male voice stopped me in my tracks.

The questioner was a cherubic-looking redhaired man, wearing a bright reindeer-patterned sweater buttoned up the front.

"I'm Alice Nestleton," I replied evenly. "Lucia's friend."

"Attorney?" he asked politely.

I shook my head. Then I knelt down beside Lucia, who still hadn't spoken. I looked up at the detective. "Why are you doing this to her?"

I could tell that something official had just clicked in his head. He opened one of the buttons of his sweater.

"You're the woman Miss Maury brought out onto the balcony that night."

"Yes."

I repeated the question he had ignored: Why was he here searching Lucia's home?

"We obtained warrants to search both her apartment and her office at Lincoln Center," he said. "For three reasons. One: We haven't been able to verify Miss Maury's account of her movements in the theater before she arrived at your box. Two: She was at the scene of the murder only seconds after it occurred. And three: She had an acrimonious affair with the deceased."

I stood up, suddenly furious at the man. " 'Acrimonious,' indeed!" I mocked him. "This is ridiculous, Detective."

After cracking a tiny smile, Wilson excused himself and went into one of the thick-walled bedrooms.

While I stood over poor Lucia, who was still too stunned to talk, I found myself, insanely, noticing yet again just how lovely the high-beamed apartment was. There were two big bedrooms, two bathrooms, an enormous kitchen, a dining alcove, this spectacular living room, and the labyrinthine hallway.

The rustling from the other rooms brought my thoughts back to Lucia's predicament. I heard muffled voices, papers being riffled, drawers opening and closing. My eye fell on a lush, fresh-cut bouquet of carnations, which stood in a crystal vase on the low antique table in front of the quilted sofa. I wondered if the police had "searched" that yet? Had they pulled out the flowers and stuck their hands into the water? The thought was absurd — and at the same time sad.

Then I walked over to the dining table, took a chair, and carried it back into the living room, where I placed it beside Lucia's and sat down.

She was still in her robe, a chocolate velour one with matching slippers. There was something equally silly and poignant about the little pompoms on the tops of her shoes.

"Can I get you something, Lucia? Shall I make a cup of tea?"

She shook her head slowly from side to

41

side. Her powerful dancer's neck tensed. I knew she was close to tears.

"You know what, Alice?" she said quietly, the tears coming now.

"What, dear?"

"I wish Splat were here. I miss him so much."

"I know," I said. "He was a delightful cat." I wasn't just humoring her. Her great, friendly Maine coon had indeed been a wonderful cat. His beautiful coat was the color of blue smoke — deep and rich and memorable.

The search party seemed to be getting impatient. We heard a closet door slam. Lucia winced. I reached for her hand and held it tightly.

"You didn't see me dance *Raymonda*, did you?" she asked.

"No, I didn't."

"Well, I was guest artist with the San Francisco Ballet that season. And the critic said I was wonderful — that I was 'graceful but not posturing.' He said my dancing 're-vealed rather than obscured.' He said, 'The key to Miss Maury's sensitivity is . . . is . . .' um . . ."

Lucia stopped the reminiscing abruptly and turned to stare hard at me. "What is happening here, Alice?" she shouted.

Her speech patterns had begun to sound very peculiar. The tones no longer seemed to coincide with the contents. It was as if she were moving further and further away from normalcy, from reason.

"It will be over soon," I said, hoping that was enough of an answer.

The telephone rang then. Twice. Three times. The noise seemed to register with Lucia, but she made no move to answer. Instead she said huffily, "I want them to go!"

"I'll get that for you," I offered, and went over to pick up the extension.

A voice on the other end barked: "Get me Wilson!"

Wilson?

"You have the wrong number," I said. But at the same moment I looked up to see the detective approaching me. *Oh, my, that is his name, isn't it?* I handed over the receiver and went back to join Lucia.

Detective Wilson listened in silence for about thirty seconds, nodding every once in a while. Then he hung up.

He came toward us purposefully, his colorful sweater now scrunched up a bit to reveal the beginnings of a classic male pot-belly.

"Miss Maury, a gun has been found. Taped beneath the desk in your office. It's a .25-caliber weapon, the same kind used to kill Dobrynin."

We all waited. I looked at Wilson, he at Lucia, she at me.

"Detective," I began, trying to make my voice sharp and authoritative. He shushed me right away.

"Do you have anything to tell me, Miss Maury?" He was focused solely on Lucia. I thought I heard a little whine escape from her throat.

"Please get dressed," Wilson instructed her. "Miss Maury, I'm placing you under arrest on suspicion of murder. I'm required by law to inform you that you have the right to remain silent, you have the right . . ."

I felt a tremendous rush of pity for Lucia at that moment, felt as frightened and helpless as I knew she felt. I hated having to listen to this stranger "Mirandizing" my old friend — it was just too much to bear. So, like an idiot, I covered my ears with my hands.

6

It was dark when I got home. I felt as if I hadn't seen my own apartment in days.

There were only a few pebbles left in the cats' dry food bowl, so I rushed to open their favorite smelly entrée. But all in all, the beasts were not at all happy about eating a midnight supper. Finally they quieted down, forgave me.

I sat down heavily on the sofa. Well, Lucia was in jail. As crazy as that sounded, it was true. Her attorney was still at the station house.

Then I remembered my visitor from what seemed like last week: Tony. I spotted the message on a ripped-out piece of note paper he'd taped to the front door. I went over to retrieve it.

Swede: The only thing you're too old for is celibacy. And too beautiful. Staying at the Pickwick Arms. Wish they were yours.

Basillio

I knew of that hotel. It was a reasonably

priced one on East Fifty-first that catered for the most part to South American tourists.

Holding the note, I sat back on the sofa. Bushy leaped up beside me. We both watched Pancho fly around my legs twice and disappear into the kitchen.

The events of the day had unhinged me. How could all this be happening? Prim and proper Lucia in jail, accused of murder. A gun found taped under her desk at work — *taped* there, something out of a gritty *policier.* I knew that she hadn't done anything wrong, but it was just as disturbing to think that someone might be trying to frame her for the murder.

After a few minutes I took an appraising look around the apartment. There was a little picking up to be done; I should sort the laundry and do a dozen other little domestic chores, but I couldn't focus on them now. On one of the chairs, in a light green binder, was a script I'd tossed there the other day and then promptly put out of my mind. My agent had described it as a black comedy, written, he said, by a woman in New Hampshire who was willing to put her own money into the production.

I drifted over to the chair and distractedly picked the thing up. The title was *The*

Bitches of Endor. I leafed through it half-heartedly. A three-woman cast. All three are inmates at a posh mental hospital called "Endor." One is bulimic. One paranoid. And the third, a catatonic who makes bizarrely choreographed gestures and lurches.

Ah, yes. The stuff of raucous hilarity. The typical Nestleton vehicle. Was it something I wanted to do? I didn't know. All I could do was just stare at the words, just pass the time — it was like mental knitting. My head was somewhere else — at the ballet, in Lucia's apartment, at the precinct house, where old iron bars threw shadows across Lucia's lovely face. The vowels on the page seemed grotesquely familiar. They seemed to remind me of the hole in Peter Dobrynin's forehead.

I don't know how long I would have sat turning the pages of that script if the telephone hadn't sounded. It was very late for anyone to be calling me. I hoped it wouldn't be horrible news.

The caller was Frank Brodsky, Lucia's attorney. I asked how she was faring.

"She'll be all right," he assured me. "We'll have her out on bail by morning."

Then he requested that I come to his office tomorrow, saying that the Maury family would very much appreciate my help. Of course, I agreed immediately.

Frank Brodsky's office was in a beautiful whitestone building in the east eighties, half a block off Central Park. I rang the bell, was buzzed in, and saw the elderly white-haired man standing at the top of a circular stair-case.

"This way, Miss Nestleton."

Up I climbed. Finally we were face-to-face, shaking hands. He was much shorter than I, but still presented an imposing picture. He was meticulously dressed in a char-coal pin-striped suit and moiré silk tie with a ruby stickpin. High above us, the sun streamed in through skylights.

Mr. Brodsky ushered me past his secre-tary and into an exquisite room that served as a study. On the walls were breathtaking Hudson River School paintings — paradisal glades and ravines and gorges. Even with my complete lack of expertise, I could tell they were the genuine article. It reminded me of the tea party I'd once attended in the garden of a wealthy widow's townhouse; I knew in an instant that the sculpture near the nasturtiums was a *real* Rodin — you just know.

We sat down at a brilliantly high-polished

table. On it were china cups and saucers and a silver coffee server filled with heady French roast. Brodsky poured for both of us, also offering me a basket of miniature rolls and marmalade. I was a little hungry, but felt I ought to decline. Wealth, power — what, stuffiness? — can have that effect on a person.

"This whole . . . *situation* is just terrible for Lucia," he began. "You and I know the charges are false. Absurd, Miss Nestleton. And we know how greatly our friend is suffering. But the fact is, if, after the ballistics tests are performed, the weapon that killed Mr. Dobrynin is proved to be the same one found in Lucia's office . . . Well, I'm afraid the grand jury will surely indict."

He sipped his coffee. "As you know, Miss Nestleton, the Maurys are quite well off."

I nodded, a little embarrassed for some reason.

"The family have empowered me with absolute discretion in defending Lucia. We need an investigator who can devote complete attention to this . . . situation. Now, I've heard that you have some experience in matters such as these."

"Yes."

"And I've heard also that, while you are a brilliantly accomplished actress, you have difficulty obtaining parts that are . . . ah . . . on your level. So that you have started a practice of . . . of . . . caring for other people's animals, their cats, specifically."

I laughed at his convoluted, patronizing, but ultimately kind way of telling me that he knew I was perpetually broke.

"I am so sorry," he said, his face wreathed with concern. "Have I offended you?"

"Not at all, Mr. Brodsky."

"Good. Well. Will you accept the assignment?"

"Of course."

"That's just fine. Lucia will be much relieved."

"Tell me, Mr. Brodsky. What, exactly, are my instructions?"

He folded his hands in front of his face, thumbs touching, as if to convey his pensiveness. That moth-eaten gesture would have invited a torrent of invective from any good director.

"You know, Miss Nestleton, I am now semi-retired. Most of the work I do these days involves trusts and estates. But I did have my share of excitement in the criminal area as a younger attorney. Believe it or not, I once defended Meyer Lansky in a tax-evasion case." He sat up a little straighter. "Mr. Lansky was acquitted, I might add.

But I am rambling. What I meant to say is that when I used investigators on a case, I found that specific instructions to them were counterproductive. That is, it was best to give the investigator free reign to explore the case. I assume that a trusted investigator is both professional and wise, and will penetrate to the heart of the matter."

"Heart?"

"Yes, the heart of the matter: Who murdered Peter Dobrynin? That is what you must find out. It is ultimately the best defense against a murder indictment of Lucia Maury."

He pulled open a drawer then and removed a slip of paper. He used one finger to push it across to me. I stared at the check, drawn on a Delaware bank and signed in an illegible hand. It had been made out to me — in the amount of five thousand dollars.

I was speechless for a moment. In an elaborate one-second fantasy I found the killer, paid all my debts, moved into Lucia's building, endowed a small theater troupe, and zipped into Bendel's to demand that the saleslady find and sell me that incredible two-hundred-and-forty-dollar straw hat with the linen flowers I'd salivated over last summer. I'd expected a token payment, perhaps. But surely everyone knew I would have wanted to help Lucia even if no money whatsoever had been involved, even if she had had less in the bank than I.

Mr. Brodsky obviously had faith in my professionalism, and I thanked him for it.

"Will you try one of these?" He motioned once more to the rolls in the wicker basket. "They're from our favorite bakery. Really excellent."

I looked at the rolls and the pot of marmalade.

"Thank you so much, Mr. Brodsky," I said, "but I'm not hungry."

7

"What's going on, Swede? You pick me up in a cab and whisk me here to glamour city. Since when can you afford this kind of restaurant?"

Basillio was hunched over, glaring at the people at the other tables. He may have been a little embarrassed at being underdressed. I had "whisked" him to a new, hyper-chic restaurant in the West Twenties. Nouvelle American, cum Southwestern, cum junk-bond traders was the way it had been described to me.

We were sipping our Zinfandel and inhaling the appetizer that had just arrived at the table — tiny braised scallops, each one covered with a dot of green paste and placed oh so artfully on the plate in a miniature forest of herbs. It was breathtaking. It cost seventeen-fifty.

"Okay, Swede," Tony said, fixing me with a smirk. "I got it all figured now. You swallowed your pride and finally took a part in a soap. And you just picked up the advance on your salary. Right? And realized at the same time that your recent coolness toward me is absurd. So now you're trying to buy my affections. You've finally admitted you're mad for my body — right? This is, plain and simple, a seduction dinner."

"Wrong on all counts, buddy," I said, after I'd ingested one of the scallops, which was pleasingly hot. "I have been retained to investigate the murder of Peter Dobrynin."

He stared at me incredulously. "You mean that crazy — the dancer who was shot over the holidays?"

"Yes."

"Why you?"

"I was there at the ballet when it happened — Christmas Eve. And an old friend, Lucia Maury, is about to be charged with the murder. Unless I can turn up something to clear her."

"Lucia . . ." Tony turned the name over on his tongue. "I don't know her, do I?"

"You may have met her once at my apartment, years ago. When I was living on the West Side."

I then told him all that had transpired: finding the body . . . the search of Lucia's apartment . . . the gun taped under her desk . . . my meeting with the lawyer Frank Brodsky.

He finished the scallops one by one, fastidiously, as he listened.

"And you want my help with the investigation?"

"Yes, Tony, I do. I think you ought to take a rest from seducing those young actresses . . . for reasons of health."

He laughed and finished his wine. An emaciated young waiter started toward the table to refresh our glasses, but Tony waved him off and did the job himself.

"I also thought," I said, "you might be able to use half of my fee — twenty-five hundred dollars. Less, of course, what this silly meal is going to cost me."

He stared at me slyly. "Now, isn't that odd, Swede? In fact, I *am* in a bit of a financial bind. The character who bought the copy shops from me seems to be going belly-up. That means the notes he gave me will probably turn out to be worth about ten cents on the dollar after the bankruptcy court finishes with him. And I'm two months behind on child support; my ex is threatening me with a long prison term. Plus, that Brecht production at the University of Texas at Austin, which has all kinds of grant money, is not going to use me. So twenty-five hundred for my body seems reasonable."

"Not your body, Tony, your brain."

"Six of one . . ." he let his voice trail off.

We had delayed ordering our main courses. But now the time was at hand. Tony called for a spicy stew of wild rabbit. I ordered brook trout with dirty rice and peppers.

We continued to drink while we waited for the food.

"I've got to be honest, Swede. I'm not a big ballet fan."

"Irrelevant," I assured him. "It's a murder investigation, Tony. Not a culture quiz."

"It's not that I dislike ballet, mind you. On the contrary. I love it."

"I think you've lost me, Tony. The logic of that escapes me."

"I'm not surprised, Watson. I'm a very subtle guy. Look — the last ballet I saw was about seven years ago. My wife had friends who used to take us. We saw Antony Tudor's *Dark Elegies*. You ever catch it, Swede?"

"No."

"Well, it was mesmerizing. I was totally overwhelmed. Literally the most beautiful thing I've ever seen. And as I watched it, I realized I was seeing the absolute definition of beauty. The music. The steps. The scenery. The mix. And then, as I sat there watching this gorgeous thing, I began to loathe myself. Because I had to admit that I could never in my life, under any circumstances, even approximate the intensity and scope of what was going on on that stage. I loved it as much as I've ever loved anything that happened on a stage. But it made me profoundly depressed. Like I said, it made me loathe myself. So I never went again."

Like most of Tony's exegeses, this was a bit much. And like all of his explanations, it held a kernel of shining truth — maybe.

We were both hungry. So when the food arrived we fell upon it and ate in happy, lusty silence. Everything was excellent. We mopped up the good juices left on our plates using hunks of (very inventive) sourdough with flecks of jalapeno. Yes, it was all excellent, we agreed a little grudgingly — even the chairs and the table and the low-key Georgia O'Keeffe colors, even the track lighting, which I usually hate — it was all excellent — and expensive as hell.

When we'd finished our desserts — I couldn't pass up the Bananas Foster and Tony had the Mexican chocolate soufflé, then we switched — we ordered coffee and brandy. We sat back in our chairs and looked around at the other diners, soaking up the ambience of the place because we knew we'd never be back here again.

Then I had to turn to serious matters. I told him what would happen next. "I want you to go to the Performing Arts library tomorrow. I'll get over to the Mid-Manhattan. What I need is a biography of Peter Dobrynin."

"You mean somebody wrote one?"

"No, no. I mean we have to construct one. The Mid-Manhattan Library has all the back issues of *The New York Times* on microfiche — all the news magazines, too. What you're going to do is go through the back issues of the dance journals. We need any and all information that will help us to flesh out the obituary."

"I'm with you, Swede. Know the character before you interpret the role. In other words, prepare."

"Exactly. And we'll meet tomorrow evening at that place on Seventy-second. You know, the one near West End."

"Right. At about seven?"

The check came then. Involuntarily, I whooped. And then I sneezed.

I spent seven heady hours at the library, armed with a large yellow legal pad and three ballpoints with different colors of ink.

There were hundreds of Dobrynin references in the various indexes. And why not? After all, he had been a star once, in the truest sense. But information on his life — other than the roles he had danced and the parties he had attended and the women he had bedded or been seen with — was very scarce.

When I arrived at the All-State Café, Tony was already there. He was seated at a table, not at the bar, and he seemed to be flushed, oddly excited.

"Research turns you on, Mr. Basillio?" I inquired, joining him and asking the waitress for a Bloody Mary without ice.

"Swede," he said, his eyes bright, "ballet critics are mad as hatters. Real perfume-on-the-handkerchief stuff. Know what I mean? They make drama critics sound like minimalists. Just listen to this effete, mumbly-mouthed crap. It's a description of Dobrynin by a critic who caught one of his early appearances in *Swan Lake*. Just listen!"

He flipped open his pad and read in mock-stentorian tone:

" 'Dobrynin was a revelation. The other male dancers displayed a pervasively forced tone that misconstrued energetic presentation for one-note pushiness. The gifted Dobrynin, however, danced like no one else onstage, gliding through long, lean, and fine *tours jetés,* and spiraling through pirouettes that stopped and finished and posed in buoyant fourth-position lunge. His moves are effortlessly silken; those of his fellow dancers, contrastingly hidebound. Fine-boned nearly to the point of slightness, powerful in his exquisite musicality, he is also blessed with a face so handsome it seems to be painted on porcelain.' "

Tony paused, his face gleeful from the recitation. "Wait! There's more. There's one other sentence that you must hear, Swede." He searched frantically through his notes, then came up with what he'd been seeking:

" 'Dobrynin's only visible weakness during this performance was that it was obvious his double *tours en l'air* were less than secure.' "

Exhausted, Tony collapsed back in his seat.

"I'm glad you enjoyed yourself so much, Tony."

"It's priceless stuff, Swede. Priceless."

I remained silent, letting his macho energy exhaust itself. Maybe on another day I'd point out to Tony that what he'd just read sounded far from "mad" to me. In fact, it had been a great deal more to the point

60

than a lot of the twaddle we'd both read about the theater.

"Hmmm, yes," I murmured in agreement. "Now, tell me, did you get any *facts,* Tony? Which is why you were there. Have any of *those* to quote?"

"A few."

Over drinks and hamburgers and shared french fries, we traded what we'd each learned that day. We went back and forth, trying to reconstruct a simple resumé of the main facts of Peter Dobrynin's life.

What we came up with was more or less this:

Dobrynin's father had emigrated from Russia to England in the 1920s. He married an American woman and then returned to live in Russia for many years as a translator for the British consulate in Leningrad. Peter, as a child, was sent to the Kirov ballet school, and became the first foreign national to be invited to join that most distinguished company.

When the family was transferred back to England, Peter danced for a while with the Royal Ballet before coming to America.

He lived in Manhattan for several years before he began his meteoric rise. And that sudden infusion of money and fame obviously unhinged — deranged — him.

Finishing his coffee, Tony ordered a brandy and said: "Well, we did a very creditable job, I think. You've got your bio."

"Not really. An aborted bio, maybe."

"In what way?"

"The three years prior to the murder are a cipher. Did Dobrynin really become a derelict? What happened to him? He knew dozens of wealthy people. If he was in trouble, why not go to them for help? Were there any warning signs that he was not just a carouser and a womanizer but an emotionally disturbed man? Who knew him best? All his fears, his intimate thoughts, his secrets, assuming he had any. You see what I mean? Dobrynin wasn't a riveter who lost his job and had to go on welfare because he could no longer support his family. There's got to be a very special story behind his winding up on that balcony with matted hair and no shoes."

"Well, yeah," Tony said. "All that's missing. But you don't expect to find that kind of stuff in the library, right? You find that out from people who knew him."

"Agreed, Tony. Very much agreed. That's why you and I are going to visit Lucia tomorrow. We've got to dig a little deeper. People usually know things they don't even know they know."

"Murderers make me nervous, Swede."

"That isn't funny!" I retorted angrily. "Lucia is *not* a murderer!"

"Okay, okay! Calm down, Miss Sherlock! You know I'll do anything . . . say anything . . . to get you to hold my hand."

I stared deeply at him then, thinking so many thoughts about crazy Basillio, worrying about him, too. Once again, I was astonished at the notion that he and I had actually been lovers. Oh, there was a lot I planned to tell him — and soon. But not now.

8

Lucia was seated on her large sofa when Basillio and I entered her apartment. However brief her imprisonment, the trauma of it was there in her face for all to see. Her skin was stretched tight and white. Her hands were restless in her lap, the fingers seeming to search for a dancer's gesture.

Across the large room sat a stranger: a handsome, diminutive black woman of middle age. She was reading a French-language newspaper.

I introduced Lucia to Tony. When she did not in turn introduce the black woman to us, my hasty assumption that the woman was a nurse was confirmed. She had been hired, I guessed, by the Maury family to keep an eye on Lucia during these stressful days.

"Your friend really looks like someone in trouble," Tony stage-whispered to me, as I left his side to join Lucia on the sofa.

I don't think Lucia heard what Tony had just said, but she looked distinctly discomfited by his presence. He remained standing, rocking back on his heels and smiling. He was wearing a nondescript sweatshirt and the kind of dark-colored trousers a bus driver might wear. It seemed that more and more these days Tony made people uncomfortable. It wasn't so much his clothing as his grin that nearly always struck one as inappropriate.

Lucia reached out for me and I nearly flinched from her touch — it was deathly cold.

"Yes, that's right, Alice," she said. "Come and sit by me, the way Splat used to do. I can just see that old thing sitting here cleaning himself."

I nodded. "Lucia, did Frank Brodsky tell you about our talk?"

"Yes, he did. I'm so grateful for your help, Alice." And her voice suddenly rose a notch. "I need your help, Alice! It isn't mine, that gun! I don't know how it got there, I swear! It isn't mine!"

"Listen to me, dear," I said firmly. "There's no need to convince me of any of that. But right now I have to find someone who knows where and how Dobrynin spent his last few years. After he . . . dropped out, lost it, if you can call it that. After he threw everything away."

"He became a derelict, obviously."

"I understand that. But he may have

65

maintained some minimal contact with people he'd known. Even if he spent most of his time under the West Side Highway."

"You don't understand, Alice, the state he was in. He was impossible to deal with. He was mad."

I paused for a moment there. "But how do you know how it was to 'deal' with him? If you lost contact with him, how do you know he was mad?"

"I know!" she spat out, with such desperate force that the woman across the room half rose from her chair.

"Lucia," I said slowly, "you told me you never saw Dobrynin again after the affair ended. Is that the truth or not?"

Lucia looked away from me. "No," she said grimly. "I saw him once more after that."

"After he'd dropped out of the ballet scene?"

She nodded, seemed to be fighting for composure. Tony, who had gradually come closer to us while we talked, now moved back a bit, as if to give Lucia air.

"He caused a terrible scene here," she went on. "It was awful. He came into the building demanding to see me. The doorman tried to question him, to reason with him, and finally to throw him out. It was just an insane coincidence that I happened to come home from the office while he was in the lobby."

"Why had he come?"

"He wanted to stay here, for a few nights, he said. He was crazy, though — shrieking and prancing about the lobby. His clothing was soiled and he smelled like —" She paused to catch her breath. "I refused him. We fought. Someone telephoned the police."

She stopped the story again, leaning forward as if she were experiencing stomach cramps.

"And then what happened?" I asked, trying my best to ignore her distress.

Lucia was crying now. "He said — after calling me the predictable names — he said I was just another in the long line of people who had loved him when he was on top, sucked the life out of him, and betrayed him now that he was on the bottom."

"Anything else?"

"No. No. He left seconds before the police car pulled up."

"Did he mention the names of the others who he thought had betrayed him?"

"I guess so." She blew her nose on a tissue the nurse had brought over to her. "I don't know — maybe." She shook her head. "He was in a rage at all of us. He probably named Melissa. And Betty Ann Ellenville. Louis Beasley. People I pointed out to you at the service."

Lucia pulled herself up from her seat on the sofa as if she weighed three hundred pounds.

The other woman approached quickly and noiselessly, then stopped at a discreet distance to wait for Lucia's next move. Close enough to assist her if she stumbled, far enough away so as not to hover or give the impression that Lucia was a cripple. I envied her her timing and tact.

"I'm tired, Alice. So tired," Lucia said. "Is there anything more now, or can you excuse me? I must sleep."

"No, go right ahead," I said. "I . . . we'll be in touch." I nodded good-bye to the other woman.

Lucia left the room at a snail's pace, the nurse matching her steps.

"She's trancked to the gills, Swede," Tony observed when they'd gone.

Of course. I'd been talking to a heavily sedated woman.

We let ourselves out and waited in the hall for one of the magisterial elevators.

"Is the game afoot, then, Sherlock?" Tony asked flippantly. "Are we about to roll up our sleeves and get *en pointe?*"

"What?"

"The game, Swede. The hunt. You know. Deduct-and-detect. Seek-and-find. Search-and-destroy. You've got the old blood lust, girl. I can see it in your baby blues."

"Enough mixed metaphors, Tony. And you know I don't have baby-blue eyes."

Ignoring me, he tried, ridiculously, to execute an ambitious ballet leap right there in the hallway. He announced it as he jumped: "Double *tour en l'air!*"

He smashed heavily into the wall, then slid down it like some hapless second banana in a Looney Tunes feature.

"Dear God!" I rushed over to the stunned Basillio and helped him up. Holding on to my arm, he hobbled to the now open elevator and stepped in gingerly.

Basillio fell into shamed silence. As we rode down, I realized there was probably more than a grain of truth in his comment about my being turned on by the "hunt." I was serious about helping Lucia out of this mess, of course, but I had to admit the idea of stepping into the *haute* world of the ballet was tantalizing in the extreme.

Unlike Tony, however, I would never be caught attempting a *tour* of any proportion. First of all — I looked over at the obviously pained and red-faced Basillio — women rarely perform that step. And second — I didn't dare let him see me struggling not to laugh — my medical insurance is always an inch away from cancellation. As for Tony's insurance, I was betting the fool had none.

9

One of my regular clients had once told me, as we sat over cups of her home-mixed herbal tea: "Put a whopping spoonful of caviar on a small piece of milk-soaked bread, and place it on the floor twenty feet away from a cat. No matter how much that cat wants that caviar, most likely she will not approach it directly — as would a hungry dog or bird or bee." Cats do not, she said emphatically, approach food directly.

"Now, there are those who say the reason for this is that the cat approaches inert food sources the same way she approaches 'live' food which she must kill to obtain — that is, circuitously, in a stalking mode.

"It is my belief that the cat is performing a quasi-mystical geometric ritual known only to felines. Which is why cats often inscribe squares, triangles, and other such configurations before finally coming close to their food dish."

At the time I had made no comment, simply taking my paycheck and saying so long to Hilda, an impossibly beautiful white angora, and Waldo, a tiger-stripe half the size of a Doberman. Yet that wild speculation on feline geometrical movements was swirling around in my head as I sat in Louis Beasley's rather strange home. He had finally allowed me to question him in his combination apartment/place of business, at 2 Fifth Avenue.

The room in which this porcine, world-famous, ostentatiously dressed impresario met me was curiously devoid of furniture, with the exception of an armchair and several writing or drafting desks, set high on swivels. Along the walls were elaborate built-in fish tanks, where colorful creatures cut like blades through the water.

Beasley sat in the high-backed armchair, a cream-colored throw over his legs.

His lover, or companion, or secretary — one doesn't quite know how to characterize the relationship in a single word — kept circling the two of us but mostly Beasley, as though the pink-cheeked older man were a potential food source. Hence my thoughts about cats and caviar. For that was what it was like: Beasley the caviar on a large and costly cracker, and Vol Teak the inscribing feline, spelling out those quasi-mystical shapes.

Beasley had been most unfriendly at the start. He'd grilled me extensively as to exactly what kind of "investigator" I was, making the word sound distasteful.

But the moment I informed him of Lucia's words — that Peter Dobrynin had spoken bitterly of Beasley's betrayal of him when he was in need — the imperious Beasley, defensive, launched into a monologue that seemed to go on forever.

"Yes, I saw him in that debased state. Three years ago this Christmas. The worst had already happened. That he had thrown away the career of the decade was enough of a tragedy. But the man standing before me had thrown away *everything* — all human dignity. Tossed it away! He accosted me on the street. I didn't recognize him at first. This great dancer . . . this god . . . this force of nature . . . there he was waiting in a doorway. Filthy. Drunk. Off his head.

"He wanted me to give him a bed!" Beasley exclaimed, the incredulity he clearly had felt that night now back in his voice. "He didn't *ask* for it. He *demanded!* He was abusive, violent. Reeking of wherever it was he'd been flopping. Why, of course I sent him away. It was simply too much to bear . . . too sad. Dobrynin had simply gone the way of all the others. And there was no way to bring him back."

"All *what* others?" I interjected.

I had affronted him mightily, I could see, by interrupting. He shone his contempt on me like a searchlight. Then, instead of answering my question, he called over his shoulder to Vol, sleek in his stone-washed black jeans and too-small T-shirt: "Perhaps it's time for coffee, yes?"

Teak nodded in affirmation but made no move at all to get the coffee.

I wished that Tony were there with me, with his disconcerting grin. At that moment I could have used his ability to throw people slightly off-balance. But he was at the hotel resting, recuperating from the stupidly self-inflicted wounds he'd suffered in Lucia's hallway.

"The other great ones, I meant." Beasley had resumed his monologue. "The great dancers, the great artists who all descend into hell eventually. Who collapse under the weight of their gifts. Whose fire of genius sets them ablaze."

Oh. I got it. That old-fashioned romantic rot that has nothing to do with the real world. But I didn't bother to protest. It was obvious Beasley himself was not a part of the real world. Rather, he inhabited one from the dim, dim past — a world long gone, if indeed it had ever existed at all.

"I can even understand," he went on,

"how that poor woman was driven to kill him."

"I'm sure Miss Maury would appreciate your understanding, Mr. Beasley, but the fact is, she did not kill him."

He dismissed my statement. "Women too numerous to count have thrown themselves away on Dobrynin. He used them like shoe-horns."

"I'm afraid I don't understand."

Beasley carefully folded up the afghan on his lap. There had been no need for it, really; the apartment was quite warm.

"Ah. But you didn't *know* Peter, did you? Your loss and your blessing. You see, he gave new meaning to the word 'excess.' He would . . . ingest . . . anything — alcohol, barbiturates, cocaine, anything. Anything that would help him slip into the desired state. And of course he always needed someone to accompany him on the ride — usually a woman. It was as if he needed someone to impress while he was getting to where he wanted to go. And of course, not to be excessively vulgar, he needed someone to . . . Well, suffice it to say that he *ate* life. And he ate people. He used women to grease the skids into heaven, and hell. You see? Like a shoehorn."

Vol's restless circling had at last ceased,

but we still had no coffee. He came closer to me, smiled — he was handsome indeed — and sat down on the carpet, executing the perfect lotus position in one smooth move.

When I had managed to pull my eyes away from his haunting face, I caught a movement in one of the tanks along the wall. There seemed to be a disturbance going on, as if the water pump that regulated the tank had gone on the blink and was troubling the placid water. Or had this strange couple installed tanks that contained victims and predators, a steady-state cycle of birth and death in which one or the other was always erupting? I almost pointed to the fish to inform my hosts of the danger, but then I let my hand drop back onto my lap.

After a moment's thought I asked, "Have you any idea where Peter Dobrynin spent the last three years of his life?"

Beasley snorted. "On the street, I presume. Or under it."

"And did it not disturb you that this . . . *god* was out there, alone, in summer and winter, perhaps starving, perhaps abused?"

"Young woman," he began — I suppose I *am* young, in relation to Louis Beasley — "I am not a sentimentalist." I might have argued with that, but I said nothing.

"Young woman," he continued, "wherever Dobrynin was, you may be sure that he was neither alone nor starving. And if there was any abuse taking place, he was not on the receiving end of it.

"In addition, the individual in filthy clothing who attacked me on the street that winter night was no longer Dobrynin the dancer, Dobrynin the god. He was an apparition. He was a hobo."

"Then you have no thoughts as to who might have shot him?"

"Well, of course I do." *Of course I do, you silly cow,* he might as well have said.

"Who?" I asked.

"Any one of a thousand women he seduced and abandoned. Any of his shoehorns."

Vol Teak spoke for the first time: "When a person degrades you, why, naturally you want to pay them back in kind," he said matter-of-factly. "Don't you think? Or, don't you?"

"I'm afraid I wouldn't know, as I've never been 'degraded' by anyone," I said, a bit prissily I'm sure. "Certainly not to the point of wanting to commit murder."

"Ah," he said, giving me a little Mona Lisa smile I hated. "Perhaps the rich can never be degraded."

"Rich? I am far from rich. So far that I'm poor."

"Well," he said patronizingly, "certainly not spiritually? After all, you *are* an actress of some acclaim, we hear."

My fifteen-minute interview with Vol Teak alone — while Beasley himself made the damn pot of coffee — had turned out to be even less enlightening — more worthless, so to speak — than the talk with the culture czar Beasley.

As I walked the cold Village street, turning around now and then to admire the majestic Christmas tree under the arch at Washington Square, I mulled over Beasley's fixation on women. Had Dobrynin never degraded *men?* Hadn't he ever used one of them as his shoehorn of the evening?

Why was it that Louis Beasley couldn't even conceive of a *man* firing a bullet into the great dancer's head?

10

Tony raised himself on one elbow. "Well, well, well. If it isn't the Florence Nightingale of the Great White Way! Is there a more compassionate woman alive? To what do I owe the honor of this visit, O tender-hearted golden angel of mercy?"

His bitterness startled me. He was obviously angry with me, but I hadn't the slightest idea why. It had, after all, been his decision to try to defy gravity. It was that preposterous attempt to execute an impossible turn that had landed him flat on his back. I reminded him of this.

"Get a grip, Basillio," I warned him. "I just stopped in to see how you were doing."

"Empty-handed? No chocolates? No roses? No *Life* magazines?"

"Sorry. I'm just on my way to Melissa Taniment's place. I have an appointment in twenty minutes." Melissa lived only three blocks away, in an important-looking dual-purpose glass building — it contained both offices and luxury condominiums — on First Avenue.

"Well, what about my twenty-five hundred? Am I still getting paid even though I'm sidelined?"

"Oh, come on, Tony," I teased. "You know I'm an enlightened employer."

He turned his torso toward the nightstand, reaching for a cigarette, and suddenly grimaced from the pain, which seemed to have become localized in his lower back.

"Still bad?" I asked.

"It's much better, but it hurts like hell when I make any kind of sudden movement."

"Why don't you go to the doctor, Tony?"

"For the same reason you don't go to a drama coach."

"Which is . . . ? Never mind, don't tell me. I don't have time for one of your philosophical riddles right now."

"So what happened with Beasley and his pet snake? Fill me in, boss."

"Nothing much. Beasley thinks Lucia did it."

"And does he know anything about our hero's lost years?"

"He says no. Says he saw him three Christmases ago, and not again until Dobrynin was in his coffin. I'm hoping Melissa will be more helpful. Unlike Beasley, she seems positively anxious to talk to me."

Tony finished his cigarette. "Listen, why don't you come back to visit me after the interview?"

"Um, I don't know, Tony. There's so much work I ought to get to today."

"Have a heart, Nestleton. Look upon me as another cat-sitting assignment. I'm a big, exotic, crippled —"

"We'll see, Tony, we'll see."

I waved good-bye and headed out the door.

Like Louis Beasley, Melissa Taniment lived in an odd atmosphere. Her apartment was an enormous modern affair, bright from dozens of windows but with the discordant feel of a mausoleum. She'd filled it with truckloads of memorabilia — ballet photos and old toe shoes enshrined on bookshelves; autographed sketches of herself done by a variety of artists; scrapbooks; and bric-a-brac, including a horrid old lamp featuring dancers cavorting on its base. The place was some sort of memory museum.

Her back ramrod-straight, she greeted me graciously. Her husband, she said, was away on business. She led me straight through the place into the big walk-through kitchen, which was spotless and cold.

I was astonished at how small she was. I towered over her. Why is it ballerinas seem so much larger-than-life onstage? I think perhaps it's their broad shoulders — the elegance of their slope. And Melissa's shoulders were impressively large, capped by a beautifully muscled neck. My earlier impression had been correct: Retirement had not dimmed her loveliness.

I flushed, suddenly embarrassed as I realized that I was regarding her as some sort of relic. In truth, she was younger than I. And I don't know that I would appreciate anyone's assessing me in the same way.

Sitting across from her, I also felt a sense of relief — Louis Beasley's characterization of all Dobrynin's women as "shoehorns" couldn't possibly be accurate. It seemed most unlikely that Melissa Taniment had ever been a shoehorn for anyone, at any time in her life. It seemed impossible that she would allow herself to be degraded.

"Now, Miss Nestleton," she inquired in a pleasant tone, "how may I help you? What did you wish to ask me?"

That phrase of Tony's — "our hero's lost years" — sprang to mind. I forced myself not to use it, however. "I am trying to discover how Peter Dobrynin spent the last three years of his life, before . . . before his untimely death. Can you tell me anything about that?"

Melissa folded her hands on the counter-top and waited a moment before answering.

"But I cannot help you answer that," she said finally, speaking with a trace, just a trace, of that affected English one picks up from speech coaches. "How could I know?" she explained gently. "We'd completely lost contact these last years."

"I see. It's just that . . . I thought he might have come asking for your help at least once during that time." It was my turn to lay on the long a's and the smile of glass.

Melissa's composure seemed not at all shaken. But I noticed that she did begin to look away from me more often. "Well, yes," she said at length. "I did see Peter once. I suppose it was three years or so ago."

"Around Christmastime?"

At last, I was beginning to pick up a faint trace of the chill I knew she was capable of emanating.

"I believe so," she said, then continued, speaking very deliberately now. "Peter demanded money from me. He was drunk, and lewd, and thoroughly abusive. My husband put him out bodily." She was staring past me by then. "That . . . is . . . all."

"He never called or tried to see you again?"

"No."

Melissa turned her gaze back to me then,

and there was something much softer in it, something almost pained.

"I did, however, attempt to reach him once," she said.

"When was that?"

"Two years ago Peter's mother died. She lived in Connecticut, near Hartford. Family friends there called me, thinking I might be able to reach him and tell him of her death. But of course I was unable to do so."

"When you say you tried to contact him — where exactly did you look?"

"Nowhere, in fact," she answered dully. "I had no idea where to begin to look for him. He was lost to me."

By now, strangely enough, her pleasant manner had begun to return.

"You see, I really cannot help to answer your questions, but I *am* happy you've come today," she said, smiling.

Now I was truly confused.

"As you can see, I don't need any more . . . things. Or money," Melissa went on. "I'm surrounded by things. But the idea that Peter left something for me is so touching . . . no matter what it is. I know I'll be grateful to have it."

"I'm afraid I don't know what you mean," I said sincerely. "Didn't Peter Dobrynin die a pauper?"

Her face congealed. "But you said you were here representing an attorney. I assumed there was an estate . . . or letters . . . or something."

"Where did you get that idea?"

The ballerina was on her feet now, and this time she seemed to loom powerfully over me. "You are here under false pretenses, Miss Nestleton! You said you were in the employ of the same attorney who represents Lucia Maury!"

"No, *you* misunderstood," I protested. "Lucia's attorney has indeed retained me, but to investigate Peter Dobrynin's murder."

"Please go!" She turned the wrath of those mysterious eyes on me.

I started to speak again.

"Liar!" she cut me off.

As I left, she spat the word again.

11

Betty Ann Ellenville had the look of the middle-aged woman who lives alone in a pretty town, spending her days doing serious organic gardening and occasionally throwing interesting pots on her woodshed wheel. She was short and pleasantly round-faced, with a careless, home-done haircut, and she greeted me in an old pair of overalls with a starched white shirt beneath the straps. No one would ever think, on meeting her for the first time, that she was one of the most respected dance critics in New York.

I had had a little adventure getting up to her loft. She lived on the top floor of a seven-story building on Spring Street, in a converted factory. I had to quickly figure out how to operate the very old-fashioned elevator that sat waiting in the lobby. One had to yank chains and pull levers and manipulate cords to get the thing moving. I felt as though I were a room-service meal going up on a dumbwaiter.

When I had finally reached her door and she had admitted me, I was delighted to see a wonderful fire roaring away in the fireplace, set in a gargantuan wall of exposed brick. It was the Soho apartment of dreams — her place was marvelous.

No sooner had she shown me to a spot on an exquisite art-deco sofa than she said, "I do not believe for a moment that Lucia killed Peter. Not for a moment. I can't understand why the police don't look for the killer among the wretched derelicts he knew. Why, he was probably murdered over a cheap bottle of wine! I mean, really! It's all quite absurd."

"I know," I said. Of course, it would be nice and neat to find the killer among the army of homeless. I chose not to point out to Betty Ann, however, that an argument over a bottle of wine would hardly lead to someone's taping a gun under Lucia's desk.

While Betty Ann went on expressing her belief in Lucia's innocence, I looked around the room. I saw over on the far wall an arresting head-and-shoulders photo portrait of Dobrynin.

"That's from a portfolio that appeared in *Vogue*," she said, her gaze having followed mine. "He *was* beautiful, wasn't he?"

I nodded. The face was aquiline. Dobrynin looked like a proud hawk, his golden hair thick and shining on his skull. It was the face of a man who could have been eighteen or forty, a timelessly handsome face that hinted at a life of debauchery — like that of many a British actor. Dirk Bogarde sprang to mind.

The few moments we sat there in silence looking at the photograph were enough to change Betty Ann's mood. Her face clouded over. It was apparent she had not yet recovered from Dobrynin's death.

"So many dancers," she said. "So many great ones. Some even technically better. But Peter was unique. You measured all subsequent performances against his. It was impossible to do otherwise. And it didn't matter who the choreographer was — Petipa or Balanchine or Ashton or . . . In a way Limon penetrated, caught his essence, more than any other —"

She stopped in mid-sentence. "I'm sorry. I'm rattling on, aren't I? You're not here to listen to my theories. You're here because of poor Lucia." She took a candy out of a dish on the coffee table. "Please, ask whatever you like."

"When did you last see Peter — prior to the funeral, of course."

"Well, the last time was a very unhappy one. A pretty ugly situation. I hadn't heard from him in over a year, but suddenly he showed up here. This was . . . oh, three years ago. He came here unannounced and I suppose he was drunk, or in some other awful state. He didn't even ring the bell. He'd gotten into the building somehow and just started up on the elevator. He got stuck between floors and started an unholy row — pressing alarms and screaming. One of my neighbors ended up calling the fire department. Lord, it was a mess. Peter attacked one of the firemen with the extinguisher that hangs in the elevator. I didn't even know who the madman was until I heard his voice. I got downstairs in time to see the police dragging him off. He was bleeding. And when he saw me he started to scream something about my being responsible for everything. Whatever that meant. He said I wanted to destroy him, to kill him. Then they took him away.

"And just to put the final, absurd cap on the story, I had a house guest at the time: my mother. It was all so grotesque!"

"And did you try to locate him after that?"

My inquiry seemed to irritate her, as if I were questioning her loyalty to the dancer; as if I too were accusing her.

She stood up and walked closer to the fire.

"Of course I would have *liked* to locate him. But what could I do? The police had released him. I tried to find him. Many people did. I even filed a Missing Persons report. But the inquiry ended when it was discovered that his mother was getting post-cards from him. The authorities said he obviously did not wish to be 'found.'

"And the truth is, he really wasn't 'lost.' People regularly claimed to have seen him. Some said they caught sight of him in the street — begging near Columbus Circle. Others, that he sometimes slept in one of those shanties in Riverside Park. It was insane. One didn't know what to believe."

Betty Ann poked at the crackling fire.

"Do you mind," I said, "if I ask a personal question of you?"

"What question?"

"Did you have . . . Did you ever sleep with Dobrynin?"

Betty Ann burst into laughter then. I stiffened, startled — and a little insulted.

She walked over to lay a consoling hand on my arm. "Oh, please don't think I'm laughing at you. Believe me, I'm not. I was just thinking of a joke people used to tell. I don't recall the whole buildup, but the punchline had to do with the technical aspect of the word 'sleep.' Peter had truck-loads of lovers, but probably very few of them actually *slept* with him. Like me."

She smiled then. "How could you spend

time with Peter and *not* have sex? He was a satyr. The interesting thing was that even though you knew it was just a throwaway for him, you weren't offended. You looked on it the same way he did — as an amusing way to pass the time. What's the phrase, 'a sport and a pastime'? He made you feel good, as if you were rendering a direly needed service."

She turned back to the photograph then.

"Peter was a little too big on throwaways, though. He went too far. And eventually he threw away his career . . . and his art . . . and his life."

I could no longer see Betty Ann's face. She had walked up to the photo and was staring at it intently.

"I really miss him. His lunacy as well as his art. Lord, was he crazy! He made a small fortune doing a series of sweater ads. Or jeans — whatever. Anyway, he went out and bought a forty-thousand-dollar Jaguar the morning after the check cleared. He left it idling in front of a bar one afternoon. And of course the car was promptly stolen. So what did Peter do? He bought another car — a jeep, for fifteen thousand. Which was towed for illegal parking. When he came out of the restaurant and found it was gone, he borrowed twenty dollars and went home in a cab. Never made the slightest effort to retrieve either of those cars." She was shaking her head as she came back to join me.

"Did he have male lovers as well?" I asked. "Sleepovers or otherwise."

"I should be very surprised if he didn't. He was an affirmative-action satyr, if you will. All were welcome."

I started to respond with a remark that might not have been in the best taste, but Betty Ann saved me from myself. She held up her hand to interrupt. "It's time I showed a few manners," she said. "I have one of those high-tech espresso contraptions. May I offer you some cappuccino?"

"To be honest, I thought you'd never ask."

Off she went. Soon I heard the fierce and bizarrely comforting sucking sounds of the machine at work.

While she was busy in the kitchen, I went over to get a closer look at the satyr. Dobrynin seemed to be looking just over my right shoulder. I wondered if his sexual liaison with Betty Ann had been the pure fun for her that she had painted it to be. Perhaps he'd looked upon it as akin to going to bed with his kindergarten teacher. I even found myself wondering whether, if I'd known him, I too would have succumbed to his blandishments, become one of his famous shoehorns. I'd always thought of myself as immune to the type. But as the song goes, one never knows, do one?

The espresso was delicious. I drained it greedily. There were still one or two things I wanted to go over with Betty Ann.

"Tell me," I said, "do you have any idea how a derelict with no shoes and no ticket could have gotten into the ballet?"

She laughed that delightful laugh again.

"My dear, haven't you ever heard of second-acting? Why, I thought you were a sophisticated New Yorker."

I told her that I was neither sophisticated nor a New Yorker. "But," I said, "I do know what second-acting is. It's how students with no money get into the Broadway shows. At the end of the first act, everyone goes out onto the street for a cigarette. When the bell sounds for Act Two, they just walk right in with the crowd. It's an old gimmick. But Dobrynin was murdered during the first part of the ballet, before there was an intermission."

"But what I actually meant," she explained, "is that there is a way to get into the ballet — as at the theater. A lot of starstruck kids sneak into the State Theater through the maze of underground garages beneath Lincoln Center. From what I understand it's impossible to get into the Met that way, but the State Theater and Avery Fisher hall are no problem for the initiated."

"And if a starstruck kid can do it, why not a canny derelict who knew the place like the palm of his hand?" I wondered aloud.

I talked with Betty Ann for another forty-five minutes — until all the hard information she had on our hero had been exhausted and her fond reminiscences took over again. I found all of it instructive.

I rode down to street level in the creaky elevator, mulling over all I'd learned. I liked Betty Ann. I found her forthrightness charming. I hoped she hadn't killed Peter Dobrynin.

12

This is where it had all begun.

I was alone in Mrs. Timmerman's apartment. I wasn't sure where the family had gone. I hadn't been paying very close attention when she phoned to ask me to come. And of course I wasn't totally alone. There with me was the object of my visit — Belle.

Belle is a white Manx. And as she hippity-hopped around the place, I couldn't help believing in the lunatic theory that somewhere, deep in the primeval past — very deep — there was a biological connection between Manx cats and rabbits.

"It's all your fault, you beauty," I scolded her as I prepared her meal in the kitchen. "If it weren't for you, I wouldn't have boasted that I could get tickets to that blasted ballet."

But she was accepting none of the blame. Nor was she concerned with eating just then. Instead, she let me know that her interest lay in playing her favorite game: kamikaze-leaping off the kitchen table and snagging Aunt Alice's stockings in the process.

Despite the occasional strafing, I liked Belle a great deal. Even if, in her attitude toward me, she vacillated between extreme friendliness and extreme enmity. But then, that could have been due to a misconception on Belle's part; perhaps she thought I was one of the Timmerman children grown up.

"Okay, Belle," I announced, sidestepping her claws. "If you're not going to eat, I'm not going to keep you company in here."

I started out of the kitchen. Then I caught a glimpse of Belle on the table, positioning herself for another jump. For the first time I realized that she was a "stumpie" and not a "rumpie." That is, she wasn't completely tailless. She had the slightest stump of a tail, but a tail it was.

"Some day I'll have to introduce you to Bushy," I said. "He's got the rest of your tail, you know."

On my way out of the apartment, I stopped to look at a framed photograph that seemed to dominate all the others atop the piano. It showed the Timmermans as newlyweds, arms linked, both dressed in summer white in front of a little stucco guest house at some unnamed beach resort. I was unaccountably touched by the sweetness of their young faces. Then I thought of the hungry strength I'd seen in the face of Dobrynin. The juxtaposition suddenly wearied me. I sat down on the flocked sofa and placed one of the small throw pillows on my lap.

I knew that I would soon have to report to Lucia's attorney on the progress of my investigation. There was precious little I could tell Mr. Brodsky. Peter Dobrynin was out of my league, out of my range of experience. All his adoring friends had loved him, they said, pitied him, mourned for him — and ultimately refused to help him. They had probably all had a sexual relationship with him. So if sex was some part of the motive for murder, any one of them could conceivably have killed him.

But so what? If Dobrynin had indeed been as promiscuous and irresponsible as everyone said, then the list of suspects might well fill up several pages on a legal pad. Any one of the dots in what our mayor had called the "gorgeous mosaic" of New York could have pulled the trigger.

As for his three lost years, if his closest friends had been unable or unwilling to find him, he must have really covered his tracks with a vengeance. If he had indeed become a classic derelict and been murdered by a peer for a motive as ordinary as a swig of

Ripple — as Betty Ann Ellenville had suggested — it was doubtful the killer would ever be found. And that was the worst possible scenario for Lucia Maury.

The pillow in my lap was brocaded. I ran my palm over the raised design. There were so many questions that kept popping up. Sure, the derelict theory was attractive, and logical in some respects. After all, derelicts do kill other derelicts. The milieu itself is violent. But how many derelicts would be able to muster the skill and foresight needed to plant a weapon so fastidiously? And even if so, why under Lucia's desk? This "derelict" would have had to have known that Lucia and Dobrynin had been fractious lovers in the past. But while I could picture two derelicts sharing a bottle on some frozen street corner, I couldn't see them revealing to each other biographical details of their pre-derelict love affairs.

Belle peeped around the corner. I waved her in. She moved up onto the coffee table, settling on Leni Riefenstahl's photographic study of the Masai. The cat's cute, near tailless rump made me smile. Somewhere in the past I had read about the number of vertebrae in the tail of the average feline. I wondered how many were missing from Belle's truncated tail.

She leapt onto my lap. "You lack a good twenty to twenty-five vertebrae, my beauty," I teased her. "Eat your heart out."

She boffed my right shoulder then, only playing — her claws were held in check.

This white-paw attack was completely harmless, but for some odd reason it resurrected the terrible sight of Peter Dobrynin's corpse. And in a split-second I realized why. White, bare feet. Clean white feet at the end of long legs, stretched out for all to see on the illumined expanse of the balcony.

I felt a surge of adrenaline.

Many derelicts go shoeless, even in winter.

But his feet were *clean.*

There was only one conclusion to be drawn: Dobrynin had entered the State Theater wearing shoes.

The murderer had removed them.

A bottle of wine was a stupid enough motive for murder. Was a pair of shoes a better one?

Or was there some much more convoluted explanation?

I had no answers yet. But that pumping adrenaline was a very good sign.

I gathered my things and scooped up the unalert cat for a kiss she rejected. "Belle, my *belle*," I told her, "there just may be a little caviar in your future."

13

I saw the little red light blinking. Only one call had come in. One was enough.

"The ballistics report has been submitted."

It was the soft, modulated voice of Frank Brodsky.

"The bullet that killed Mr. Dobrynin on Christmas Eve was fired from the weapon found taped beneath the desk in Lucia's office. A .25-caliber, semiautomatic, Czech-made handgun."

The attorney had spoken the words calmly, as if he were a TV newsreader forecasting mixed clouds and sun.

I felt a little sick to my stomach. I looked unhappily at Tony, who had hobbled along with me to Brodsky's office. But Tony seemed more interested in the impressive array of Hudson River paintings than in police ballistics reports.

"There is no doubt in my mind that the grand jury will indict now," Brodsky pronounced. "And given the circumstances, it will be for Murder One."

"What circumstances?" I asked, a bit too aggressively, almost as though the lawyer and I were not on the same side. Then I tempered my response with: "After all, Lucia says it isn't her gun. She doesn't own a gun."

He went on, in even more measured tones. "Ah, but the weapon — the *murder* weapon — was found in her office, *secreted* there, the prosecution will say. And of course there was, how shall we say, a troubled history between the two. The grand jury will be made aware that Lucia and the dancer had a romantic involvement years ago. That the affair ended badly. They'll say Lucia brooded and became increasingly despondent — and vengeful. That she lured Mr. Dobrynin to the theater and murdered him there.

"Given these factors, and given the predisposition of juries to be severe in their judgments of people with wealth and power, the grand jury will surely find premeditation."

He pronounced the word "premeditation" as if he were borrowing it from another, more vulgar, language.

"And so," Brodsky continued, "your investigation becomes even more crucial. The process must be stepped up, if you will."

He smiled at me and at Tony, as if in deference to our newly declared importance. An awkward silence ensued, until I realized the attorney was simply waiting for my report.

But what did I have to report? That I had constructed an incomplete biography of the victim? That it looked as if the murderer had made off with Dobrynin's shoes? I didn't think that was what Mr. Brodsky wanted for his money — or rather, Lucia's money.

"I've interviewed several of Dobrynin's closest friends," I started. "They all paint a picture of a talented man of insatiable appetites — and utterly out of control."

"Does any of them appear to have had a motive for killing him?"

I paused before answering and looked at Tony, who was grinning at me. He and I both realized from the attorney's question that he had no idea what kind of person Peter Dobrynin had been.

"Motive? Oh, yes," I said. "They all might have had a motive, I suppose. From what I've learned, virtually everyone who had any intimate dealings with him grew tired of him, or grew to loathe him, or fear him. He was promiscuous in every sense of the word. He used people. He . . . degraded them."

The lawyer had no immediate response to that. Instead he poured himself half a cup of coffee and motioned that we should help ourselves to some.

Then he asked, "What about the line of inquiry you were following? The years in which he dropped out of sight. What have you found?"

"Not very much," I admitted. "Just random stories of Dobrynin appearing briefly and then going back underground. Unsubstantiated sightings of him. And plenty of speculation. I think the only thing we can treat as fact is that he lived a sort of derelict existence on the West Side."

"How will you proceed now?"

"Well, Mr. Brodsky, I've only scratched the surface of Dobrynin's life. I plan to contact some of the dance companies he was affiliated with. And to find out more about his financial affairs. I thought I would now develop an in-depth profile of —"

Frank Brodsky held up his hand, interrupting me. "We haven't time, Miss Nestleton. Lucia has no time."

"I understand how pressed for time we are, Mr. Brodsky. But you cannot expect immediate results."

"I do not. But I would think your focus — our focus — now should be not on Mr.

Dobrynin himself but on Mr. Dobrynin's assassin. Don't you agree that the quickest path runs through the derelict brier patch?"

"I don't know that I do agree, Mr. Brodsky. But I appear to be in the minority. Virtually everyone I spoke with is on your wavelength. They believe he was killed by another homeless person."

"Quite. And so?"

"So?"

"So it appears, Miss Nestleton, that the best course might be to search out his derelict acquaintances."

"That's not as easy as it sounds, Mr. Brodsky. I mean, homeless populations are constantly shifting. Many of those people are addicts, criminals, released mental patients."

"Yes," he answered simply.

"And I don't know that I'm really equipped to conduct that kind of investigation."

"Why not? If I may ask."

"For all kinds of reasons, Mr. Brodsky."

"The potential danger, for instance?"

"There is that. But that isn't the only reason I'd prefer to go about the investigation in my own way."

Brodsky gave me another patronizing smile, but this time I saw the glint of steel behind it. "I think, Miss Nestleton, that if you are not presently 'equipped,' as you put it, then you should become so. Don't you agree that, given Lucia's predicament, any other course would be frivolous?"

I was stung by his criticisms and his manner. So much for the leeway he had claimed he would give me, the trusted professional.

"One other thing," he continued.

"Yes, of course, Mr. Brodsky."

"I've set up an expense account for you and your associate, Mr. . . . Mr. . . ."

"Basillio," interjected Tony, who had been circling the room up to now, paying not the slightest attention to what was going on. I had a most compelling urge to slap him across the face. But if Brodsky thought I had botched things before, I could imagine how he'd respond to my attacking my own colleague.

"Yes. Mr. Basillio, of course. As I was saying, a special fund has been set up to enable you to buy information from people on the street who knew Dobrynin — *if* you can locate them."

Another barbed comment, I thought.

"I am certain Mr. Basillio can guarantee your safety, Miss Nestleton. As I'm sure he must have done countless times in the past."

Tony chuckled appreciatively. I glared at him, but he didn't notice.

The problem was, I just wasn't ready for the kind of enterprise Frank Brodsky wanted to launch me on. Yes, certainly time was of the essence. He was right about that. And yes, I had accepted a huge fee for my services — five thousand dollars. But mine was a more intensive, cerebral style of investigation. Searching out arcane facts . . . making connections no one else seemed to recognize . . . unraveling knots . . . unearthing supposedly irrelevant tidbits of data . . . extracting the truth from among the ambiguities. Yes, it was that kind of inquiry that played to my particular strengths. It was not easy to see myself acting like an undercover street cop. But that was what Brodsky expected of me, apparently.

I looked over at him. He was waiting patiently. Waiting for my decision. Clearly, it was going to be his way or no way.

Tony was standing up very close to one particular painting — a magnificent rendition of a mountain gorge and waterfall, set in a festival of jagged cliffs.

Then he limped happily over to the two of us, exclaiming, "I've actually been there!" He pointed back excitedly at the painting. "That's Lookout Mountain! In the Catskills!"

Brodsky and I both regarded him dumbly. I felt my face go hot. When the attorney made eye contact with me again, I noticed for the first time that he had lovely blue-green eyes. And they seemed like the eyes of a young man.

Basillio continued, oblivious to our lack of response, "I've always loved this kind of stuff. It almost makes you dizzy — like good brandy."

"Well," Brodsky replied, this time looking searchingly at Tony, "perhaps one day you will have the good fortune to own one, Mr. Basillio."

Tony laughed heartily and hobbled back to his chair.

"No, Tony," I said. "Don't sit down. I think we have our instructions now. We can let Mr. Brodsky get back to work." And then I said directly to the lawyer, "I will do my best."

"Excellent," he said quietly, watching us go. "That's excellent."

I'd agreed to stop for coffee and strategy-planning with Tony — in fact, I'd suggested it. But the explosion I felt rumbling in my chest wouldn't hold long enough for us to reach the café. So I began shouting in the middle of the sidewalk.

"Basillio, if you're going to fall apart from your mid-life crisis, then so be it! But if you *ever* humiliate me that way again in front of a client, I will *kill* you! *Understood?*"

Tony turned frightened, perplexed eyes upon me.

"Quit the 'Who, me?' act, Basillio! What the hell was that nitwit art-lover act all about? Didn't you notice that Brodsky thought you were a moron? And don't you see how behavior like that reflects on me? That it makes me look ridiculous?" I felt tears welling up in my eyes and angrily fought them down.

Tony's face crumpled then. "I'm sorry, Swede."

"So am I!" I barked. "I'm sorry you're in trouble and I didn't see it sooner. But I have a client — and a very old friend — in trouble, too. Lucia's going to be sent to prison if we don't do something, Tony. Prison!"

"I understand that," he said.

"Do you, Tony? Do you really get that?"

"Yes!" he said, his own anger rising, then fading. "I just said I did."

"Then, do you think you can hang in there with me until this is over? Because if you're going to cave in, Tony, then . . . then . . . ," I said hopelessly, "then I don't know."

He took me by the shoulders. "It's okay, Swede. It's going to be okay. I'm going to report for white knight duty, same as it ever was. You'll see."

I began to relent.

"And I'm really sorry if I lost it in front of whatsizname — the Claude Rains guy."

"Patronizing old man . . ." I muttered.

We said we'd talk about "it" — "it" being whatever worries or demons seemed to be stalking Tony these days — when we got to the coffee shop. But we didn't. We talked about the case.

14

I'd given Basillio a couple of early-morning assignments. Then he was to pick me up at my apartment. It was close to ten A.M., which meant that he was forty minutes late. Resisting the panic that prickled just under the surface of my skin, I stood at the window leafing through that crazy script. Finally, the downstairs bell rang.

"Sorry I'm late," he said, rushing through the door. "But it wasn't my fault. It took forever to set things up at the bank. And then the photos weren't ready when I got to that place on Twenty-third."

He put two brown envelopes on my long living room table and then blew on his whitened fingers.

"Why aren't you wearing gloves, Basillio?"

"I never wear gloves. They inhibit the sense of touch."

"What are you touching on the street?"

He shrugged in answer.

I undid the buttons of his pea coat and loosened the muffler around his neck. "Don't get overheated, sport."

I picked up the larger of the two envelopes and opened it. There were supposed to be thirty-five ten-dollar bills inside it, taken from the special expense account Frank Brodsky had set up. I felt the heft of the stack of bills, as if I could determine whether the money was all there just from the weight. It felt right, I guessed.

Then I looked inside the other envelope. There were five different shots of Peter Dobrynin, taken from newspapers and magazines and reproduced in wallet-sized prints. All were late photographs of Dobrynin, which was good. But unfortunately, none of them equaled in clarity of feature the photo I'd seen in Betty Ann Ellenville's loft. On the other hand, how could they?

"Want some coffee, Tony?"

"I want many things. But I'll settle for java."

I went into the kitchen and turned the flame way up under the kettle, returning with a cup of instant Medaglia d'Oro for him.

"I won't be long," I said. "Just let me get on some socks and a pair of warm sweaters. I mean, some sweaters and a pair of — you know what I mean."

I went into the bedroom to dress for the

long, wintry walk on the wild side. When I came back into the living room I saw Tony, seated backward on a chair, staring intently at Bushy.

The cat was basking in his daily circle of light — a spot by the window where a small but brilliant beam of sunlight appeared each morning. It wasn't there for long, but before it dissipated it was as dazzling as any diamond. Bushy's burnished coat gleamed in the sunlight, his eyes half-closed, his body still and expectant. He gave the impression of a king sitting for the royal portraitist.

"What are you doing?" I asked Tony good-naturedly. "Admiring the gorgeous Mr. Bush?"

He gave a disgusted snort. Then his face contorted slightly as he began to speak in a grossly broad "mitteleuropa" accent. I realized at once that he was gracing us with his not-very-good Peter Lorre impersonation.

"Your cat may be quite beautiful, madame, but . . . heh-heh . . . I denounce him as a traitor and a fop . . . heh-heh . . . To you perhaps he is an innocuous Maine coon. But we know him to be an imposter, a fraud. Why, he cannot catch a mouse or a bird . . . or, heh-heh . . . even a cricket. And for his crimes, I say he must die. . . . I must *kill* him . . . heh! I *want* to kill him." He then hobbled out of the apartment door, and I followed.

I know Bushy heard it all, but he never moved a muscle.

We chose to start at Forty-third Street and Ninth Avenue, walk north along the avenue until we reached Roosevelt Hospital, then go east to Broadway, up Broadway to Seventy-second Street, and west on that street until we hit Riverside Park.

This route, we hoped, would provide us with maximum exposure to the homeless people who existed in the shadow of the Lincoln Center complex and who might have known Dobrynin.

At the beginning our progress was impeded by the sheer numbers of homeless — in alleys, on gratings, in the entrances to banks where the cash machines were located, anywhere these people could escape from the cold. We were also impeded by our reluctance to confront these unfortunates, because of their dress, their demeanor, and often their smell. Then too, as we needed to show the photographs to them and get some sort of coherent response, our total lack of experience in differentiating between the merely down-and-out and the mentally deranged was a real liability.

But it really didn't matter. No one responded to the photos anyway. And no matter how we tried to resist that kind of behavior, we ended up handing out many of the ten-dollar bills just for charity's sake — which was awfully bad strategy.

We stopped to drink coffee at a little muffin place on Fifty-seventh Street, walked another block to the hospital, and were about to head toward Broadway and the Columbus Circle area when Tony spotted another candidate pushing an enormous makeshift wagon heaped high with his belongings and detritus of all sorts. There were newspapers and sprung sofa cushions and books and rags, all tied onto the contraption with twine.

The heavy-laden man was approaching us from uptown, perhaps heading toward the small public park at Ninth Avenue.

"I think we've got a hot one," Tony mocked. "Let's show the dear boy to him."

As we drew closer to the man, we took in his bizarre costume. He was wearing a black ten-gallon hat with a few greasy feathers attached to it, and a filthy buckskin shirt with long, bedraggled fringes. He appeared to be a buffalo-hunter who had emerged from a hundred-year sleep. His grizzled whiskers only buttressed the image.

Tony stepped up to the man and politely addressed him. "Excuse me, could I speak to you for a moment?"

The old-timer halted, eased the end of his cart to the pavement, and met Tony's gaze with an open, if blank, expression of his own. "Hell, yes," he answered. "You can speak, buddy."

"Have you ever run into this man?" Tony displayed three of the pictures, fanning them out like playing cards.

The buffalo hunter squinted hard at the photos.

"Say, partner, you wouldn't happen to have a smoke on you — while I'm looking them over?"

Basillio lit one of his cigarettes and handed it over. The derelict seemed to crush down on it with his lips and puff out smoke in great billows.

He "looked them over," as he put it, for quite a few minutes. I thought he'd forgotten we were standing there. But presently he brought his eyes up and, flicking his fingers contemptuously against the head shot on the left, said, "Never liked him. Never liked that one at all."

"Are you saying you know him?" I burst in.

"Hell, yes, I know him," he said. Then he took on a menacing air. " 'Buddy,' I told him, 'keep movin'! Get movin' and keep movin' — see? 'Cause I don't like you!' " He gave out what I'm sure he meant to be a hard-bitten laugh.

Tony quietly extracted two ten's and stuffed them with emphasis into the breast pocket of Buffalo Man's shirt.

"Can you tell us when you last saw him?" I asked.

He puffed on the cigarette again like a mad whale, then said, with true reflection: "I believe the last time I saw Lenny was Thanksgiving . . . over there at that dinner they give us. At the soup kitchen."

"Lenny?" I repeated. "Did you call him 'Lenny'?" Basillio and I exchanged looks, suddenly deflated.

"Hell yes, it's Lenny. Oh, hell yes. He tried to hang around, but I told him, 'Keep movin'!' Just moved him along. Never liked him."

Tony retrieved the photos and displayed them once more. "Are you sure that's Lenny?"

Buffalo Man picked them out of Tony's grasp and spent less than two seconds studying them again. "Lenny," he pronounced, handing them back.

"Tell me," I said before he could move on. "Where is this soup kitchen? Where you last saw Lenny."

He seemed surprised that the where-abouts of the soup kitchen wasn't known to all. But after we had apologized for our ignorance, he told us all about the kind people at the church on Seventy-first Street. Then Buffalo Man picked up his overburdened cart and left.

Tony and I stepped into a doorway to warm up a bit and to digest our first investigative success.

"I don't know, Tony," I said. "How can we be sure that Lenny was Peter Dobrynin?"

"Well, that guy seemed positive."

"But he may be totally psychotic."

"I doubt that."

"But why would he call himself 'Lenny'?"

"How should I know?"

"I think we'd better go over to that soup kitchen."

The custodian was the only one on the premises of the Episcopal church. The man pictured in the photos didn't look familiar to him, and he didn't know anyone named "Lenny." In addition, he told us, the church had suspended its feed-the-homeless program about six weeks ago, due to lack of funds. He did give us the names of the churchgoers who had run the program, though. We thanked him and left.

On the street again, Tony complained, "Not being a hardy Nordic type like you, Swede, I can feel the energy draining right out of me. This cold weather really takes its toll."

"You mean you want to call it a day?" I asked. "I probably shouldn't have you out here in your crippled condition, anyway."

"No, I'm fine. But I do vote we dip into those tens to buy us something to eat."

I hesitated only for a minute. I was indeed hungry — and cold.

Tony guided me to an old-fashioned family-style Italian restaurant. He hadn't been there in years, he said, and though I'd probably passed it dozens of times, I'd never even noticed it before. We were coming in at an odd time — between lunch and dinnertime — so it was absolutely devoid of customers. The waiters sat drinking coffee together at a large round table. Tony and I took a booth and ordered opulently: a good Chianti; a Caesar salad for two; antipasto for two; then pasta. At the end of it all, we shared strawberries with zabaglione.

The food took its time in getting to us, but

we didn't care. We were warm, and being fed very well, if very slowly. We'd already had a long day, and it wasn't over yet. I felt I was earning my keep, even though it was impossible to evaluate the little we had learned so far.

For if Buffalo Man was not totally crazy, then we had at last hit upon something solid. Dobrynin had indeed consorted with the homeless. He had been one of their number, known to them as "Lenny." Unknown to them was the fact that "Lenny" had been the premier classical dancer of the past decade. It was all quite surreal. I was deep in thought, deep into the whole Dobrynin phantasm. The sound of Tony's laugh brought me back around.

"But it was a lot of fun, wasn't it, Swede?" he said.

"What was fun?"

"The endless hanging around, walking around we did in the old days. Remember how we'd do a bar, then a coffee shop, then a movie, then something else? How even going into a department store was some kind of adventure? We'd ride the elevators and just observe people. How the hell did we end up doing so much walking in those days? And here we are, more than twenty years later, wearing out the pavement again.

Why did we do it, Swede?"

"Haven't the slightest idea," I said tersely. I wasn't sure why, but I wanted to nip his nostalgia trip in the bud.

But I did know why. I remembered.

Basillio and I had entered the theater when the acting schools were still under the sway of the Stanislavki Method of acting. The major premise is simple: You construct each part out of the felt traumas and joys of your own life. If the role you're playing calls for the character to cry, *you* cry, by remembering the pet who died when you were a child. In that way you infuse the part with authenticity. Obviously, then, you're only as good as your experience. The more traumas the better. The more joys the better. The more you have suffered, experienced, the better an actor you are, and the wider your range.

In short, a good actor has to be "wilder" than a non-actor. And believe me, we believed it. My determination at that age to live fully — highs, lows, sex, love, work, pain, empathy, scholarship — was awesome. I was going to be great.

The American version of the Method is dead now, but the myths associated with it are still alive, if in a rather pathetic way. Hollywood stars who are making millions construct biographies of themselves to show

how close to the edge they've lived — to prove that they were truly wild once upon a time. Whereas in fact the only wild thing about them is that occasionally they leave their Brentwood home with only one bodyguard.

That had been the purpose of those endless walks of Tony's and mine: to gather up people and things and feelings like bouquets. To see more, feel more, learn more, exult more. Everything we encountered on those walks was a memory to be stored away and used on the stage.

I looked across at Tony, smiled at him. But I was surprised to see him glowering, head down, eyes boring into the empty plate in front of him.

"Basillio, what's the matter?"

It was a long while before he raised his eyes and addressed me, with a disturbingly unfriendly look on his face.

"There's something I want to ask you . . . Alice."

I was stunned by his use of my given name, but managed to reply, "Ask away."

He didn't ask the question right away, but idly picked up the utensils on the table and began arranging and rearranging them.

Then he said, quietly, gravely, "Why don't you love me?"

I thought it was a bit. I laughed.

"What's so goddamn funny!" He slammed a fork down on the tabletop so viciously that wine from his glass sloshed out onto the little dish of sugar packets. "Sorry," he said, straightening his back.

"Tony," I began nervously, "I don't know what to say. I thought you were perfectly happy impressing your young actresses. A lot of men would love to have your success at —"

He cut me off. "I pick up actresses, Swede, because you seem to have no interest in me anymore."

"Tony, that isn't true and you know it."

He ignored me. "You have no interest in me, even though everything I've done these last couple of years has been because of you. If it hadn't been for you, I wouldn't have left my wife — well, maybe that wasn't totally because of you. Maybe that was coming, anyway. But I left *when* I left because of you.

"And if it hadn't been for you, I wouldn't have gone back into the theater. Which hasn't exactly been easy, Swede. I have about as much chance of making it as a stage designer now as you have of finding Peter Dobrynin selling pencils on Columbus Avenue.

"Plus, you give me mixed signals. On the

one hand you like having me around to help out with your work. On the other hand you shut me out of other things in your life. On the one hand you sleep with me once in a while. On the other, I'm highly expendable. I can be replaced, and I know it.

"So where do I stand? Huh? That's why I want an answer to that one lousy question: Why don't you love me?"

But rather than wait for an answer, he went on making his case.

"I'm a smart guy — right? Imaginative? Oh, I know I'm crazy, but I'm not dangerous, right? I'm crazy in an interesting way. We like the same things — the same actors, the same plays, the same food. And best of all, I . . . *know* you. I know how you feel, I know how you think, I even know *what* you're thinking usually. So what the hell else is there? What's missing?"

He leaned close to me, the pain so clearly etched in his face that I had to look away.

"So, Alice" — his voice was low and hoarse — "why don't you?"

"Because, Tony," I said at last, "there's love . . . and there's love." And that's all I could manage. I reached across the table and took his hand. Nothing more to say. But I knew I would take him home with me that night.

"I think that was the best night I've had since 1978," Tony said sleepily.

The early-morning light looked muddy as it came in through my small bedroom window, more like the residue of the sun than the real thing.

"What happened in '78?" I asked.

"Oh, I don't know."

He reached for me under the blanket.

"It was great, Swede. We got it right, didn't we?"

"Um," I said.

I looked into Basillio's eyes and smiled indulgently. I have never understood some men's compulsion to rate sex, as if it were just another ball game with scores and hits and errors. Sure, it was good. But wasn't it supposed to be? It was exciting and tender and all that. But there was no reason to quantify it, was there?

His hands were warm against my skin, moving, tightening. "I think we're on a roll here, Swede," he said, mouth close to my ear. "Let's start the day right."

I thought about it for a second. "Let's not," I said gently. "Time to get to work."

I felt a thump at the foot of the bed. Sitting up, I was astonished to see Pancho regarding us — more accurately, regarding *Tony* — closely.

It would not have surprised me in the least to see Bushy there; after all, he often slept with me. And in fact, hurt that someone had supplanted him in my bed, Bushy had spent the night in the bathroom, next to the heating pipe. But Pancho! He had never sat still long enough to learn the pleasures of warm covers.

"Panch, what *is* it?" I asked.

His yellow eyes were fixed on Tony, gleaming madly.

"Is he going to kill me?"

"Don't be silly," I told Basillio. But Pancho did look almost lethal sitting there, the muscles in his flanks and shoulders twitching from time to time. Is it possible, I found myself musing, that Pancho believes Tony to be the enemy who has been pursuing him all his life in my apartment? The cause of his perpetual flights through the house? Is it possible that, having cornered his pursuer at last, he's going to turn the tables on his enemy?

"Tony's a friend," I assured the cat, and reached out to stroke Basillio's head.

But whatever Pancho had been planning, my sudden movement spooked him out of it. He flew off the bed and went zooming down the hallway.

"Your apartment is getting dangerous, Swede. Wonder how many guys have been trapped in here and eaten alive by that monster. And what does the vain one do — watch?"

I made coffee and brought it to Tony in the shower. Over breakfast, we laughed a lot.

By nine o'clock we were at the Seventy-second Street entrance to Riverside Park. This ribbon of a park, which stretches four miles along the Hudson River, from where we stood up to Trinity Cemetery on One Hundred Fifty-third Street, has long been a haven for homeless people. They tend to congregate at the intersections where the park widens to absorb traffic circling onto Riverside Drive: at Seventy-second, Seventy-ninth, Eighty-sixth, and Ninety-sixth streets. In these sections of the park, there are labyrinths of tunnels and slopes and rock outcroppings.

The first two hours of our investigation that morning were futile. We talked to ten or twelve of the homeless, most of them staying warm in cartons or lean-tos under the viaduct at Seventy-second Street. None of them recognized the photos we showed them.

Our luck changed as we walked north on Riverside Drive. A fat man was panhandling at a bus stop around Seventy-fifth Street. He was doing it in a unique fashion. He had propped himself up against the bus shelter with the help of a single crutch, the better to expose one very ugly, swollen, and battered leg to the passersby. In his hand he held a styrofoam coffee cup, which jangled with change as he shook it. The exposed leg was supposed to induce sympathy, and it couldn't have done otherwise — it was truly a horrible sight to behold.

The portly man was wearing one of those woolen stadium caps, on which was printed SAN DIEGO CHARGERS. He was a long way from San Diego. His beard was ragged and dirty and he wore several vests, randomly buttoned. His eyes were bloodshot, and there was a stench of sour wine about him.

"Excuse me, do you know this man?" Tony asked him, trying to keep a safe distance from the infected leg while still getting close enough to let the man get a good look at the photos. The fellow plucked one from Tony's hand, turned Dobrynin's face upside down, then said "Nope" and grinned nastily.

Angry, Tony pulled the photo away from him, righted it, and gave it back — this time accompanied by a ten-dollar bill.

The fat man stared at the money for a minute before pocketing it. "Lenny used to give me a fifty," he said contemptuously.

"What?" Tony said, foregoing caution and edging a bit closer to the man and his leg.

"You knew Lenny?" I asked.

"He even used to give me a hundred sometimes."

Another crazy turn in this crazy case. When Dobrynin had dropped out, he might or might not have gone around the bend. We didn't know for sure. But everyone agreed that he had been broke. Yet if this man was to be believed, our "Lenny" had gone around handing out hundred-dollar bills.

The fat man only sighed when we pressed him for more information about Lenny. "Don't ask me," he dismissed us. "Talk to Fay. She knows more than I do."

Fay, it turned out, "lived" near the boat basin. He pointed us in that direction, telling us to say that Harry had sent us. "Yeah, Harry," he repeated impatiently. "That's me. Just ask Fay." And he went back to rattling his cup, the vile, puffy leg still shamelessly exposed.

We hurried along. Because it was winter,

the only boats moored at the basin were houseboats. On the benches that lined the walkway to the water dozens of men lay sleeping, eating greasy lunches, smoking, drinking from bottles in paper bags. They all knew Fay. One directed us right to the hillock on the northern limit of the docking basin.

She was seated on the frozen ground, on folded newspapers. Next to her was a banged-up shopping cart filled with her possessions — or at least that's what I assume they were. The sheer bulk of the cart's contents was overwhelming. I didn't study them very closely.

In fact, seeing Fay in another context, one might not have known immediately that she was one of the army of homeless. She was clean, quite presentable, but there was something discombobulated about her appearance nonetheless, and she wore a frightening amount of rouge. Her coat appeared to be a real fur, in decent shape, but upon closer inspection I could see that its collar had been taken from some other garment and haphazardly sewn on. On her feet were plush-lined bathroom slippers — odd enough in itself, considering the temperature — but under them were wildly mismatched men's socks.

There was no question that Fay had known Lenny. The minute Tony flashed Dobrynin's photograph, her eyes lit up in recognition. And in something else — love, perhaps. She took the photo and held it close to her cheek, almost cooing his name.

"Lenny! I've been waiting for him," she said breathily. "Where *is* Lenny?"

We lied to Fay. Tony invented a story about Lenny's having been hit by a car. We were old friends of Lenny's, trying, he improvised, to gather some background information to help an attorney sue the driver of the automobile. Lenny would be well in a few months, Tony said. He was on the mend.

Fay's distress at the news shamed me. But I couldn't tell her the truth.

"I hope he gets back soon," she finally said. "His babies are hungry. I don't have the money to feed them."

That one really stumped me.

"What babies are you talking about, Fay?" I managed to ask.

"*His* babies!" she replied brusquely. "He always gave me the money to buy food for them. Delicious food. Oh, he takes good care of those babies. Sends me over for the best stuff. Chicken Kiev's their favorite."

Basillio was taken with a violent coughing

fit. He turned his back to us for a minute.

"Lenny gives me the money," Fay continued, "and I go over to that Russian place to get their food."

"You don't . . . by any chance . . ." I asked haltingly, "mean . . . the Russian . . . Tea Room? On Fifty-seventh?"

"Yes," she sniffed. "What do you think I mean? Grand food he gives them. And us, too. Lenny feeds us all. Now you just tell him those babies are hungry."

When I asked her to take us to the babies, Fay was reluctant. "What for? You wanna hear 'em crying?"

A couple of our ten's got her on her feet. Tony had handed me the money wordlessly, all the time shaking his head in wonderment.

We were led across the hillock, through one of the small stone tunnels that dot the park, and emerged in front of a large rock outcropping surrounded by an iron rail fence. Here we came to a halt.

"See any babies?" Tony asked me. "I don't."

Fay began to rummage around in her cart. At length she pulled out a huge stainless-steel spoon, something that I guessed they were still looking for at one soup kitchen or another.

She stepped up close to the fence and pulled the spoon noisily along the rails. It made quite a racket. She stepped away from the fence and smiled at us.

There was a blurry movement on the rocks on the other side of the fence, and then a big, battered tomcat came into view. He approached the fence slowly, as if each step were a hardship.

Then another cat appeared, this one a dingy calico. Then another. And another. They began to arrive in pairs after that. They kept coming and coming, in an unhappy procession. They all looked cranky and underfed. All expectant.

"See?" Fay said without satisfaction. "There's all the hungry babies. See 'em?"

"Swede," Tony whispered to me, "I don't think we're in Kansas anymore. This is the last straw."

I only half-listened to him. I was paying more attention to Fay, who went on, "And tell him the other ones are hungry, too. The ones up at a Hundred and Third. Tell Lenny we need some money right away."

The desolate cats set up a wailing chorus.

"Oh, I can't stand it when they cry!" Fay whined, stuffing the spoon back into the cart and starting to move off. She called back to us, "You tell Lenny, if he can't come out here to leave some money in his apart-ment! I'll go and pick it up!"

I rushed over to her, keeping up with her surprisingly energetic pace. "Just a minute!" I said. "Lenny has an *apartment?*"

Fay snorted. "Now look here, sister! Lenny is a gentleman! You ever know a gen-tleman who didn't have a place? Why, he's got a mansion! A big, blue mansion. I know . . . I been there."

Out of the corner of my eye, I saw the cats slowly moving off. The signal for food had sounded. They'd been called to supper. But they were going away hungry.

15

While Fay was giving me directions to the "blue mansion," Tony just stood nearby, whistling to himself. When I told him where we were off to he said this whole thing was getting insane, but I insisted we go looking for the apartment, which was reportedly on upper Broadway, on the border of Harlem.

We stopped at one of the many new watering holes "gentrification" had brought to the vicinity — this one at One Hundred and Twelfth Street. Tony wolfed down a hamburger while I had soup. The barstools were plush and comfortable, and the place was soothingly lighted. A jukebox in the back was playing a woman vocalist's unusual — in fact, downright acidic — version of the old classic "Stay as Sweet as You Are."

Tony's skeptical head-shaking had only increased by then. It was as if he had a mosquito trapped in his ear.

"I know, Basillio, I know," I told him. "We're in Never-Never Land. But you said you were going to stay with me on this."

"I'm staying!" he protested, chuckling. "I'm staying."

We sat drinking for a while.

"You know what's bothersome?" he asked a few minutes later. "I mean, what *else* is bothersome, putting to one side our close encounters of the third kind today."

"What?"

"Isn't it weird how all that stuff his so-called friends said about him is turning out to be worthless?"

"Explain what you mean," I said, sipping my Bloody Mary, which was too sharp for my taste.

"Well, for openers, they all just *knew* that he had been a homeless derelict for the past three years. It turns out he had an apartment — excuse me, a 'blue mansion.' "

"We don't know that for sure, not yet, anyway. We'll find out in a few minutes whether Fay was telling the truth about that."

"Humph. And what about the money? The money everybody said he didn't have. The friends told you he'd squandered it all — didn't have a dime — that he hit them up for money. But he had enough for a mansion. He had enough to buy cat takeout from the Russian Tea Room!"

"You've got a point there, Tony."

"And the way they all said he was an egotistical maniac, a user who lived only for his own perverse gratifications, whatever the hell they were. Turns out he went out of his way for some of these . . . poor unfortunates. Lavishing chicken Kiev on a gang of stray cats, for god sake! Sounds to me like he was on his way to sainthood."

I nodded, not sure whether he was right on that last point. After all, as every actor knows, people are endlessly complex and contradictory. One trait does not a whole character make. A man can, theoretically, be a self-involved bastard yet still care about stray animals.

I gave up on my drink and ordered a cup of coffee. I thought of the cats in the park who had so suddenly appeared when Fay rasped that spoon across the railing. For some reason I couldn't bring myself to believe that Peter Dobrynin had been the Mother Theresa of the feline world just because he'd fed them expensive Russian cuisine. I don't know why I felt that way. Maybe because stray cats who live in the park always do better than strays in abandoned buildings and alleys. It's the latter whose existence is so sad and so problematical, so filled with terror and danger from vehicles and starvation — and heartless people. Those are the cats I wish he'd seen to first. There are countless numbers of them only a block outside the park. And they certainly don't need gourmet food; all they need is commercial cat food.

Thinking about all the strays made me depressed. Over the years I had spent hundreds of hours with various short-lived volunteer programs, trying to rescue stray cats. It's hard to catch the poor things, even those who are hurt or emaciated. And once you catch them it's harder still to find homes for them, unless they're kittens. And if you can't place them — what then? Give them to the animal-welfare agencies? That often means death. I finished my coffee and pushed the cup away. If I stayed in the bar I would begin to remember specific strays. And I didn't want to do that.

Tony and I walked uptown on Broadway, past the Columbia University campus, past the seminaries and music schools. We crossed under the elevated subway station on One Hundred and Twenty-fifth Street, then turned west on One Hundred Twenty-sixth.

It was a dingy street of squat factory buildings one right after the other. I looked searchingly up the block. Then I heard Tony say, "Well I'll be damned."

We saw the blue building. At least, it had once been blue. The paint had come away from the brick in great hunks, and the structure was now a speckled blue-and-rust.

We entered through double steel doors and found ourselves in the small lobby, aged marble all around. The old building directory indicated that there were only two tenants remaining in the place: a metal-spinning firm on the second floor, and an auto-parts wholesaler. It didn't appear that anyone lived in the building, just those two industrial tenants.

"What are you doing here?"

Tony and I whirled to the right, where the voice had come from. A gray-haired man in taped-together spectacles stood inside the open fire door. He was holding a plumber's snake and some other implement I couldn't name.

"Who are you?" he demanded, coming near us.

"Who are *you?*" I retorted, sounding equally suspicious.

"I'm the super," he said, gripping the tools more tightly.

Tony spoke then, pleasantly. "We're Lenny's friends."

At that the super relaxed, even treated us to a smile. Obviously, he liked Lenny.

"Where's he been?" the super asked. "Haven't seen him in a while." Then a worried look crossed his face. "Something happen to him?"

Tony launched into essentially the same story he'd made up for Fay's benefit. "Well . . . yes," he answered, serious but not overly grave. "There was an accident. He's in Beekman Hospital, downtown. But he'll be okay."

"Oh. Sorry to hear that," the man said. "Lenny's the best tenant I ever had — except when he brings those bag people around sometime."

"Yes," Tony went on. "Lenny's good people. He really cares, doesn't he?"

I decided it was time for me to jump in. "I'm so relieved we were able to find you. Lenny didn't have a thing on him when he was hit. No keys, no money, or anything. He wanted us to pick up a few clothes and things for him. Could you . . . ?"

The super set his things on the floor, extracted an outsized ring of keys from his back pocket, and led us up the stairs. When we'd reached the third floor we walked down a gloomy hallway, at the end of which there was a solitary door.

"Right here," the super said, trying one key and then another until he'd found the right fit. He pushed the door open, switched on the light, and told us he'd meet us downstairs when we were ready to leave.

Basillio and I were equally dumbfounded by what we saw before us.

The room was brilliantly lit by a series of spotlights overhead. The floor, a beautiful parquet newly waxed and shining like a gem, had been coated, it seemed, with a gripping agent.

Dobrynin-Lenny had fitted the room out as a ballet studio, complete with a practice barre and a mirror that ran the length of one wall. There were two towering armoires in the room — both filled with leotards, toe shoes, leg-warmers, sweatpants, all sorts of dance paraphernalia — as well as a stereo system and a shiny black grand piano.

"Curiouser and curiouser!" Tony mumbled as he looked around.

I walked along the opposite wall, looking at the mats and blankets scattered on the floor. No doubt, the bag people the super had mentioned stayed over once in a while.

"Swede, look at this!" Tony called. "There's a video here in the VCR."

I went over to join him. He was grinning. "I wonder what kind of stuff your friend liked to watch."

"He wasn't my friend, Basillio. I never met the man."

Tony flicked switches to turn on the TV

and set the videotape in motion. A moment later a couple appeared on the screen.

"Now, why doesn't this surprise me?" he said, leering.

It was obviously a home-made video, shot, it quickly became clear, exactly where we were standing. The man and woman on the tape both had beautiful bodies — dancers' bodies. And they were both completely naked.

"Is that the great Lenny . . . or should I say, Dobrynin?" Basillio asked, his eyes riveted on the screen.

"Yes," I said.

The couple were dancing now, fluidly, wonderfully. It was eerily beautiful. I found myself shivering.

"Know who the woman is?"

I didn't answer.

Tony looked up quickly at me, then turned back to the television set, his face up close to the screen. "Who *is* it, Swede? And what are they doing?"

I recognized what they were "doing," thanks to some of those long-ago rehearsals I'd attended with Lucia Maury. They were dancing one of the early scenes from *Giselle*. Giselle and Albrecht execute four *ballotés* and then a *balloné* and a *grand jeté*. I could almost hear the old rehearsal mistress

141

calling out the steps.

"Come *on,* Swede," Tony demanded, his voice full of urgency, as if the video were disturbing him in some way. "Do you know who that woman is or not?"

"Her name's Melissa Taniment," I said.

16

"How do you get an outside line?" I asked.

We were in Tony's hotel room, having taken a cab back from Lenny's strange "mansion." I was still a bit dazed by what I had seen. I had to call to Lucia now, had to find out more about Melissa Taniment. As an insider, Lucia would know all the intimate details about her — even the salacious ones, I hoped.

"Dial nine first," Tony instructed.

He was seated in the easy chair in front of an old, feebly hissing radiator. One leg stretched out in front of him, he was gingerly rubbing it. Obviously the heavy amount of walking we'd been doing lately hadn't furthered his recovery from the fall he'd taken trying to execute that ballet step.

Over the ringing at the other end of the line, I could hear Basillio say from behind me: "You know, Dame Nestleton, your basic problem is that, deep down, you really are an academic. You should be teaching somewhere — teaching the finer points of acting to a group of eager young know-nothings. The fact of the matter is that you're a little too decorous for your own good. The fact of the matter is that you would never dance naked with me. Never in a hundred years. Even if it wasn't being videoed."

I found that amusing. "But Tony," I said, "you're not Dobrynin. Who knows what I might have done if *he* had asked me to dance?"

No response from Basillio. And none at the other end of the line. I hung up finally and called Frank Brodsky.

The attorney told me that Lucia was at home but taking no calls. She was falling apart, heavily sedated and under the care of her physician. The tension had just become too much for her.

I escaped from his questions about the investigation as soon as I could, saying I had a pressing appointment related to the case.

Then I phoned Melissa Taniment. I identified myself and said it was urgent that I see her again; might I drop by for just a few moments?

She informed me that she had no wish to see me this evening, or any other.

"Are you willing to put that response on videotape?" I asked.

I waited out the long, loaded silence emanating from the other end of the line, until she said stonily, "Come over now." Then she hung up.

"Do you want company?" Tony asked.

"No, you stay here and rest. It won't take long. I'll bring back some soup for you," I offered, getting into my coat.

"Sure. Tell him to make the soup straight-up. And with two olives in it."

I left the hotel and walked directly to the glass tower. Melissa didn't say a word as she opened the door. Obviously she had just emerged from the shower — there was a huge blue towel wrapped around her head and she was wearing a bathrobe of the same color.

Parking me once again in the kitchen was her way of telling me that I was déclassé, not worthy of a seat in the living room — like a repairman. I transferred a copy of *Harper's Bazaar* from one of the kitchen chairs to the table and sat down.

Melissa went over to the counter, on which stood one of those elaborate juicers that seem capable of pulverizing anything into liquid nothing — even aluminum cans, if one wished to add them to the brew. Next to the contraption were oranges and carrots and what I took to be mangoes — all lined up for the eventual slaughter. She began by quartering the oranges, still ignoring me completely. I waited in silence. She moved on to the carrots. Neither of us spoke. Finally, she dropped the knife disgustedly onto the counter and sat down across from me at the table.

"You were in his apartment," she said bitterly, fearfully.

"Yes. And I watched the tape."

She sat rigidly in her chair. I could see that she was trying to collect herself. She looked down at her hands on the tabletop, willing them to be still.

"It isn't true, is it, that you hadn't seen Peter Dobrynin during the last three years of his life? You lied when you told me that."

Her eyes blazed. "Of course I lied to you! I owe you nothing!"

I only smiled a little. "Please go on," I said.

"Oh, for god sake, what do you want me to say? That I went there once a week? I did. Sometimes more than that. That I made love with him? Of course I did. There — does that satisfy you?"

"You did something else," I said. "You danced."

"Yes," she admitted petulantly, "but only once . . . like that. He . . . made me." She folded her arms suddenly across her chest, as if she were chilly. Then she leaned toward me, her face suddenly that of a child pleading with its mother.

"Please. Give me that tape. I will pay you anything you ask. Please!"

Her offer of a bribe made me uncomfortable. But she had good reason to attempt to bribe me. If I gave the tape to the police, they would be very interested. If I gave it to the papers, they would resurrect the case and splash her face — and possibly a lot more than that — all over page two. In any case, she would become a suspect in the murder. And, probably most threatening of all as far as Melissa was concerned, her social lion of a husband would know everything.

I kept my eyes on the juicer while I pondered her predicament. Finally I said to her, "I don't want your money. But I *will* hold the tape until the murderer of Peter Dobrynin has been caught."

"She *has* been caught!" Melissa retorted angrily. "Lucia Maury killed Peter."

"I don't think so. In fact, at this point you're a much more likely candidate than Lucia."

"I was at a dinner party on Long Island the night Peter was killed. With five other couples. How could I have killed him?"

"I don't know — at the moment. But there are ways."

She exploded in fury. "I loved him! I always loved him, you ridiculous woman! Do you understand that? I would *never* hurt Peter in any way!" She was screaming the words out.

I waited a second for the storm to pass, then asked dispassionately, "Were you giving him money?"

"No. Never. He never asked."

"Then where did he get his money?"

"I don't know."

"Were you aware that he was spending a fair amount of money feeding stray cats?"

"He may have mentioned it once or twice."

"And did you consider that odd?"

"No. Why should I? He liked animals of all kinds. And besides, he was always doing impulsive things, things other people never understood."

"Why did he start to call himself 'Lenny'?"

"How should I know?"

"Are there any other compromising videotapes?"

"No. Not with me, there aren't. I never wanted to do it in the first place. It was so childish. But Peter insisted. He was drunk. And maybe I was too. It was so embarrassing dancing that way — nude — in front of his friend."

"Friend? Who was that?"

"The man who filmed us. He operated that damn video camera."

"Can you give me his name?"

"I think it was Basil."

I sat back and tried to make something of this new bit of information. None of Lenny's street acquaintances had mentioned someone called "Basil."

"Was he a homeless man?" I asked Melissa.

"I'm not sure. Probably. He came and went. All I knew about him was that he was an ex-convict. Peter seemed to like that, for some reason. It was almost as though he was amused by the fact that this man was a criminal."

"What was he in prison for?"

"I have no idea. Peter never told me — and I didn't want to know."

"Can you describe him?"

Melissa sighed in exasperation. She stood up, adjusting the blue towel around her damp hair, and moved back to the counter. She hefted the knife again, but made no move to cut more ingredients for the juicer. I had a moment's awful fear, thinking she might turn the knife on me.

But all she did was turn it over and over in her hand. "Listen to me," she said tightly.

"I don't want my husband to find out. He *mustn't,* do you hear? He is a very good and kind man, but he would never . . . I told him that things between Peter and me were over long ago. He wouldn't understand."

No, I bet he wouldn't, I silently affirmed.

"Did you ever see anyone else in the apartment?" I asked next. "Anyone at all — men, women, anyone?"

She grimaced, her expression telling me that she was well aware of Dobrynin's lunatic promiscuity. But also, curious about where the question might lead.

"Are you referring to anyone in particular?" she asked cagily.

"Well, perhaps Betty Ann Ellenville, or even Louis Beasley . . . or Lucia."

"No. I never saw them. He had cut himself off from people like them. I told you — I only saw that Basil. Oh, and once or twice an older woman, another street person, I assume, who apparently ran errands once in a while. She looks a fright."

"Is her name Fay?"

"I'm sure I don't remember."

"But Basil you saw fairly regularly?"

"That's right."

"Please tell me what he looks like." The question I had asked earlier, which had not been answered.

"He's a light-skinned black man. Tall. Very thin. He speaks with an accent — a Latin accent of some sort — maybe Cuban. And he has a pencil mustache."

"Anything else?"

"Oh, God! Can this *please* be over soon?" Melissa virtually threw herself back into her chair.

"In just another moment," I said. "Are you sure there isn't anything else about Basil?"

"He usually wears a blue raincoat," she said through her teeth. "Without buttons. He keeps it closed with a belt from a pair of trousers."

I left a few minutes later, but didn't go straight back to the Pickwick Arms. I stopped off instead at the first place that caught my notice — luckily for me, a lovely little French café across the street. I needed a few minutes alone, not just to collect my thoughts but also to shake off the emotional aftereffects of Melissa's incivility. The cappuccino was a good, strong restorative.

The sudden emergence of this "Basil" was unnerving. Maybe even more so than the discovery of Dobrynin's living quarters, or the *Giselle* tape.

Until the gun was found in Lucia's office,

many people connected with the case had believed that Dobrynin was killed by another derelict. If the police hadn't found what they were certain was the murder weapon, as well as its owner, they surely would have mounted a manhunt for Basil once they'd come to know of him.

I remembered what my old friend Detective Rothwax had once told me: "The reason you irritate so many professionals is that you seem to have no respect for the 'statistical nut.' "

When I'd asked him what that term meant, he explained it in simple language. If there are two suspects in a murder investigation, he said, and only one of them has a past felony conviction, the odds are greater than a hundred-to-one that the ex-convict is the murderer. And it is upon the ex-convict that the police must focus.

It was a simple rule, crude really, but obviously tried-and-true in routine crime investigations. I smiled into the steam of my coffee. One thing was sure: If I wanted to find Basil quickly, I was going to need Rothwax's help — statistics and all.

17

Frank Brodsky had listened attentively to my report. He found Dobrynin's cat-feeding activities "amusing." The hidden apartment he thought "strange and intriguing." The videotape featuring the dancer and Melissa Taniment he thought "regrettable, sad." But Basil was "the most important breakthrough in the case" — the discovery of a real-life derelict with a prison record.

Tony was at his most dignified. He sat with a small notebook in his hands, making a real effort not to be distracted again by Brodsky's prized collection of Hudson River School art.

"You're to be commended, Miss Nestleton. You've done very well very quickly," Mr. Brodsky complimented me. "Lucia is lucky to have such a friend looking after her interests."

Brodsky's careful, pear-shaped words annoyed me. And clearly there were some things he didn't understand. He seemed to think that Lucia and I were the best of friends, an intimate, ongoing part of each other's lives. Not true. Of course we'd known each other for years, and liked each other. But we hadn't been close friends for a long time.

And in truth, she had never been the kind of friend to me that Barbara Roman had been. When Barbara died and everyone said it was suicide, I had felt compelled to take the case out of my deep love for her. With Lucia and her current trouble, it was just a bizarre sequence of events that had brought me to this juncture: I had happened to be cat-sitting for a lady who wanted tickets to *The Nutcracker.* I'd contacted Lucia to get the tickets. Peter Dobrynin was murdered the very night I attended the performance. One thing had just followed another.

The lawyer was also wrong about the commendable job I was doing on this case. Yes, revelations had been coming at an astonishing rate lately. But neither my intelligence nor my diligence had had much to do with their appearance. I was merely following in the footsteps of the departed Dobrynin/Lenny — and he had been such an unpredictable, charismatic, terrible, fascinating character that all I'd had to do was bend down and pick up the revelations like so many daisies.

"Do you think you will be able to find this man Basil?" Brodsky asked.

"I'm going to get some help," I said.

"From whom?"

"A city detective I know named Rothwax. We used to work together."

"In the police department, you mean?"

"Well, yes and no. I was employed briefly as a consultant for something called RETRO. It's an independent computer unit within the police department. It deals, or tries to, with major unsolved crimes. This detective has been of help to me in the past."

"Good," he pronounced. "That sounds like a fine idea. Keep me informed."

I wondered what on earth Basillio could be writing in that notebook.

I met Detective Rothwax in a dim sum café south of Canal Street, about four blocks away from the RETRO office. He looked pretty much the same, albeit a couple of pounds lighter perhaps, a bit balder, a bit friendlier.

"It's nice to see you, Cat Woman. Been a while. I often think fondly of our stakeout at that kooky garden over there in the East Village."

"Surely you're not holding *that* one against me, Detective? I gave you the arrest of your life — a fugitive bomb-throwing killer."

I looked down at the indecipherable menu on the table in front of me.

"So you did, CW, so you did," he replied. "Say, let me have that," he said, taking the menu away from me. "Am I paying or are you?"

"Oh, you're paying, Detective."

"Then I'll do the ordering."

As he talked to our waiter, I noticed there was a difference in Rothwax's appearance. It was his clothes. They were much less shabby. Oh, he had always worn a shirt and tie and suit jacket, but before now they had tended to look like something he'd stolen from a dead bank teller.

Now he wore a soft heather-gray suit with a spiffy patterned red tie, and his overcoat, which lay folded over an empty chair, was cut in the sharp-cornered Italian manner. Rothwax picked up on my scrutiny of his clothing. His eyes twinkled.

"Checking out my new image, are you? Like it?"

"Yes, Detective. Very much. Is there a promotion or something in the air? What does it mean?"

"Nothing at all. A bad joke. I've been assigned to work some OC cases and I just felt like getting into the part. We theater people know all about that, don't we?"

I didn't understand. "What is an OC case?"

"Organized Crime. RETRO has expanded."

The first few dishes arrived — dumplings of all kinds in steamer baskets, on plates, in egg cups. I had no idea what the protocol was. Which should you eat first? Which was what? So I followed Rothwax's lead and went methodically from one item to the next. It was all delicious. We chatted amiably as we ate. He became expansive, telling me the latest rumors about RETRO and its chief officer, Judy Mizener.

"I want you to know, Cat Woman, that you're still a legend at RETRO. I mean, every time somebody sees a mouse, we say, 'Call Alice Nestleton.' " He enjoyed his little joke immensely.

I had decided long ago to take in good humor whatever teasing of me he handed out. I often need him. I certainly trust him. And, oddly enough, I like him.

Finally, stuffed from the meal, he looked at me slyly in that way he has — head down, eyes rolled up as if peering over the top of spectacles — and asked: "So what is this meeting all about?"

"I need a little help."

"That's my cue," he said wearily, and whipped out his spiral-bound notebook, already turned to a blank page. I filled him in on the case. From his suit pocket he took out an old simulated-ivory fountain pen and uncapped it.

"Name?" he asked, pen poised to write.

"Basil."

"Is that the first name or the last name?"

"I'm not sure."

He looked at me incredulously. "Okay. What was he in for?"

"I don't know."

"Uh-huh . . . Federal or state?"

I shook my head.

"Did he do the time in New York?"

"Well, I don't —"

"Aw, Cat Lady!" he moaned. "What *do* you know?"

"That he was released from prison recently, maybe as recently as six or eight months ago. I know his street name is Basil. And I have a fairly detailed description of him. Also, I know the general area where he was last seen."

"Not enough for a computer search," he said. "Can't help you."

"Then what do you suggest I do?"

"How important is it to find him?"

"Very."

He stared at me as if trying to evaluate my need, my seriousness. Then he sighed and looked around. "I could've sworn this place had a pay phone."

There was one, just inside the entrance. I pointed to it.

Rothwax pushed out of his chair. "Two quarters, please."

I burrowed into my coin purse and produced them.

"Where is it that Basil hangs around now?"

"Upper West Side."

He went away.

He was back in five minutes. He tore a sheet from his notebook, folded it, and handed it to me. "The addresses of three halfway houses," he explained. "If your friend got out on parole there's a good chance he went to one of them. Even if he ain't there now, he probably passed through. Do some legwork."

Rothwax said there was a special dessert he wanted me to try — a custard. That banal word hardly did justice to the delicate and singularly good hot concoction that I was soon eating. I loved it.

We spent the rest of his lunch hour making fun of our respective careers. Rothwax adored actresses.

The morning started out so successfully it

took my breath away. But, as my grandmother used to say, "It is always the sweetest butter that goes rancid first." Cynical old dairy farmer that she was.

At ten-thirty in the morning, I stood waiting outside while Tony went into the first of the halfway houses that Detective Rothwax had identified for me. This one was two blocks from the river, on West Ninety-first Street, near Broadway. Tony found Basil almost immediately, seated in the television room. Soon afterward, the two of them were walking toward me.

Melissa had given an excellent description of Basil, accurate in every detail, down to the shabby blue raincoat. Up close, he was older than he first appeared — at least late middle-aged. And his face had that thinness and hunger and sharpness that one usually associates with addicts.

Tony signaled me that he had already given Mr. Basil some money. I introduced myself and told him that I was seeking information about Lenny from those who had befriended him.

"Everything about your articulation is dishonest," Basil replied.

His words, and the way he spoke them, induced a kind of bewilderment in both Basillio and me. Melissa had said he was possibly a Cuban and didn't talk very much. Well, this strange character was no Cuban, as far as I could tell, had no Latin accent, and seemed to be almost theatrical in his presentation.

"First of all," Basil spoke again, "we both know that Lenny is dead, so you really can't know anything about Lenny anymore. He doesn't exist. That entity called 'self' has vanished . . . unless of course you believe the self survives bodily death. You arc a beautiful woman. Tell me, do you believe it?"

I didn't know how to answer. I hardly knew what to do at all. While I stood there, dumb, Tony made the suggestion that we all have a hot chocolate together. Why not?

The coffee shop was overly warm. Basillio and I peeled off layers of sweaters and scarves. Basil seemed completely at ease. He looked around happily, his gaze finally settling on me. And an unsettling gaze it was. He began another strange monologue: "Besides — or shall we say, in addition to — your original statement was false, because Lenny was no friend to me."

"Oh, really?" Tony interjected. "I heard you were his *only* friend."

"He was, God rest his kindly soul, my employer."

It was during this last bit of declamation

that I thought perhaps — just perhaps — I had heard a bit of an accent in his voice. But certainly not Cuban. More like Cockney.

Our drinks arrived. Each hot chocolate had a mound of artificial whipped cream floating on its surface.

I had finally found my own voice. "Could you please," I asked Basil, "explain what you mean about his being your employer?"

"Could you please," he replied, doing an eerily good imitation of my own voice, "distribute another gift?"

Tony extracted another bill and handed it over. Basil slipped it into his pants pocket.

"Why is there need to explain?" he asked loftily. "Union against labor. Master against slave. Beauty against beast. White contra black. What need to explain, your ladyship? Lenny employed me on his staff. Or rather, I *was* his staff."

"In what capacity were you employed?" I asked.

"Collector," he said promptly.

"Collector? Of what?"

"Cash, your ladyship. Money. Scratch. Capital. Coin. Modes of exchange."

I could see that Tony was about to repeat that last nonsensical phrase, "modes of exchange," but my hand on his arm stayed him.

162

"Please tell me about it," I urged Basil. I indicated to Tony that he should get out another ten-dollar bill. "In detail."

"My master required me to write a message on the wall of a building."

"Any building?"

"No, bitch. Only one building. At 1407 Broadway."

"And why did you write this message? Who was it for?"

"I'd write the message. Twenty-four hours hence — or sometimes forty-eight hours — a big black car would circle the building looking for me. Long-haired white lady would stick her hand out the window with an envelope. I relieved her of it, and brought same to my employer quick as jackrabbit."

"Who was this lady?"

"She never graced me with her face."

"How do you know there was money in the envelope?"

"The same way I know that a bear will relieve himself in the great outdoors."

Tony handed over a bill all on his own initiative then. It's true, I too had begun to appreciate Basil's antics.

"Let me ask you now," I said. "What was this message you wrote? And was it always the same one?"

"Always. I put 'Anna Pavlova Smith.' "

My God! The name clanged in my head like the bell on a runaway trolley.

Anna Pavlova Smith?

It was the graffiti painted on the side of the hearse during Peter Dobrynin's funeral.

Suddenly, Basil wasn't so amusing.

"Were you the one who did that?" I asked Basil resentfully.

He turned to Tony then. "What thing has Miss Thing just requested?"

"Did you paint that name on a hearse — at Lenny's funeral?" I demanded.

"Not I. I've copped to painting a building. Over and over. Always on the downtown side. But a hearse? No. My credentials are impecunious."

I was silent for a moment, as I tried to decide whether I believed him. "Why always on that one building?" I finally asked.

"Ask my employer."

I glowered at Basil. In a very short time, I had gone from fearing him to appreciating him to loathing him. Worse than any of that, I believed him. It was all so mad, but I did believe what he'd told us.

Basil struck me as being entirely capable of murder. But Dobrynin had apparently taken care of his collector. Why kill the "employer"? To take over the extortion scheme himself? I didn't think Basil had that particular kind of ambition. I had to find out who the extortion victim was, and what Lenny had had on that person. And as for that name, Anna Pavlova Smith, what did it mean, and why was it popping up again now, like a bad show tune?

I pushed the gummy hot chocolate away untouched.

"You are a beautiful woman," I heard Basil say. "Have you ever worked under the name of Guinevere?"

I met his wily stare but did not reply.

"Perhaps you used to work the Knights of the Roundtable?" he inquired, as he rose and took his leave.

Was he indeed wily? Or was he crazy?

Through the glass at the front of the restaurant I saw him belt his raincoat and walk into the wind.

It didn't seem odd that Dobrynin had befriended him.

18

"You really think Basil did it?"

Tony went on to answer his own question. "The guy seems more tragic than dangerous. More victim than assassin." Suddenly he sat up straight and snapped his fingers. "You know, actually he looks like a man who'd be happy designing sets for prison plays."

I was seated cross-legged on my living room rug, close to Bushy. We were playing one of our games — S & G, for "stare and glance." There really was no purpose to the game. No one won or lost. It was just a playful way to pass the time. We would stare at each other. Then turn away. Then just glance at each other. Turn away. The idea was for one to catch the other giving a look out of sequence. A mindless game. But I know that Bushy knows I'm playing a game with him, and that's good enough for me.

Tony had started to pace. I took my shoes off and noticed that the bottoms of my jeans had become frayed. *And in the role of Raggedy Ann, ladies and gentlemen, may we introduce Miss Alice Nestleton, the forty-one-*

year-old vagabond-manqué. Tonight's episode:
"Ragamuffin on the Run."

"What are you smiling at, Swede?" Tony had been observing me while I was spinning out that fantasy.

"Nothing."

"Well, get your mind back on the case," he said teasingly. "I've been thinking about that stupid message Basil had to write on the building. What does it mean? And why always on *that* building? You think maybe the woman in the car lived in the neighborhood?"

"I don't know. But at least we know how Dobrynin supported himself in the style he was accustomed to. He was blackmailing someone."

Tony objected. "You can't make that assumption. In fact, it seems more like some kind of drug deal was going down — or maybe payment for stolen merchandise. The graffiti could have been a signal that he had the goods, and the mysterious lady could have been paying off."

"Ah, but when and where was the merchandise — or drugs, or whatever — delivered? Why wouldn't Lenny have had Basil deliver that? Basil said he was a *collector*. He never said he *delivered* anything."

"Well, I guess," he agreed.

Tired of S & G, Bushy ambled away. I lay down flat on my stomach.

"You want to hear a very odd coincidence, Tony?"

"They're my favorite kind."

"I'm pretty sure that 1407 Broadway is at Fortieth Street."

He considered it for a minute. "Yeah, it is. I know because when I used to gamble some, before I became a born-again set designer, I went there once or twice when I won a big bet at OTB. The main administrative offices of New York City OTB are in that building."

"That's nice to know," I said sardonically. It wasn't very likely that I would ever have to visit the off-track betting offices. "But the coincidence is that I believe 1407 Broadway was built on the site where the old Met Opera House once stood, before Lincoln Center was built."

"Yeah . . . so?"

"Well, of course the old Met is said to have been one of the great stages of the world, and virtually every major foreign ballet company that visited the States would appear there."

"Right. But Dobrynin wasn't old enough ever to have danced there."

"I realize that. But his mind was so

strange, he may have chosen that building simply for its nostalgic value."

Tony halted his pacing near the window. He turned around and made an expansive gesture with his hand, as if he were putting the final flourish on a painting. Then he began to laugh. "Imagine the numbskull, big-budget musical somebody's bound to do a few years from now. They'll call it *Lenny* — no, that title's already taken — they'll call it *Dobie!* And they'll hire me to do the sets.

"I can see it now. Think on this, Swede. The curtain opens on a darkened stage. A single spot illuminates the wooden backdrop. There's canvas, miles of light yellow canvas, stage left. And on it is painted an enormous erect phallus emerging out of a bed of toe shoes."

Tony whooped with laughter.

"What's the matter?" he asked me when he'd calmed down a little. "Don't you approve?"

I hadn't really joined in the laughter because Tony's mythical set for *Dobie!* came too close to what I had been feeling about the life and death of the great dancer and satyr.

"I like the idea very much, Tony," I said. "As a matter of fact, I think it's rather brilliant. And it *is* believable. I think Dobrynin was murdered because of sex . . . or rather, love. Love denied or love perverted or love skewed. And I think Melissa Taniment may have had him murdered."

"But wait. You believe that she loved him, you said."

"That's right. I do. I also believe that he was blackmailing her, threatening to tell her husband about the affair."

"But if he was blackmailing her all that time, why would she keep going to him? Week after week after week, for years. How do you make love to someone who's extorting money from you? It makes no sense."

"Maybe sense has nothing to do with the kind of passion she had for Dobrynin," I countered.

"Well, it definitely is true that this case isn't long on sense. But from what you've told me about Melissa she's too desperate, too fragile to do something like that. Sounds like she spends her time pressing flowers into books. Isn't that what happens to ballerinas, anyway? Too much deprivation, too much discipline, too many hours of practice — it cooks their brains."

He paused, then added, "Besides, we have no evidence."

"Yes, we do. We've got the videotape," I said forcefully.

"That's not evidence. That's just soft porn."

"Maybe not. Maybe there's more in it than we realized. Maybe we didn't watch it carefully enough."

He cocked his head and stared suspiciously at me. "Wait a minute, Swede. Are you telling me you want to watch that tape again right now?"

"I am."

"We've got a few problems with that. First of all, the tape's back at the hotel. Second, we would need a video-player to watch it on. And third, you don't even have a TV."

I stood up, walked over to him, and gently stroked him behind one ear, as I would Bushy. "Wrong on all three counts, dear Basillio," I said gently. "First of all, your hotel is a short cab ride away. Second, we can rent a VCR at the video store on Third Avenue. I did it once before, so I know how to connect it. And last, I do have a television. It's in the kitchen, on that small rolling table, with a dish towel draped over it."

He grumbled, thought for a moment, screwed his face up in martyrdom, cursed under his breath, looked around for help . . .

but didn't actually say another word until he had his coat on and was halfway out the door.

"Here," he said. "This is for you. I found it a few weeks ago and keep forgetting to give it to you."

He handed me an old color Polaroid print, then closed the door behind him.

I looked down at the snapshot. It was almost twenty years old. It had been taken at some sort of party. Three people appeared in the photo — Tony, me, and Saul Colin, then director of the Dramatic Workshop, where Tony and I had studied. Colin stood between the two of us, holding on to each of our arms.

In the photo, I wore an ankle-length black velvet dress cut very low in front, with puffy sleeves. Around my neck was a choker made of jet. My hair was long and golden and very shiny. I stared at the camera straight on, playing the role I always played back then — mysterious, profound, daring, available, distant. At the time that photo was taken, many men were in love with me. I tried to recall whom I'd been in love with then. I couldn't.

That poor snapshot made me terribly uneasy. I didn't know why. I took it to the hall closet and buried it deep inside one of the shopping bags that held the family memorabilia my grandmother had bequeathed to me.

Tony came back with the rented equipment and the videotape just as it was beginning to get dark. We watched the tape in the kitchen, standing close together.

The entire dance sequence was only eight minutes long. Because this time I was watching with a purpose, I picked up on various things about the production that had escaped me the first time around. Why, for example, had they decided to dance without music? It seemed almost willful, as if they wanted to disassociate the steps from music.

The tape was just as erotic as ever. In fact it sent a funny kind of chill down my body . . . tentative . . . expectant . . . tactile. After all, the two naked people on the tape were two of the finest dancers in the world at one time — and while age had diminished Melissa's skill as a dancer, and debauchery hadn't helped Dobrynin's, they were still remarkable. And they were dancing one of the loveliest pas de deuxs in ballet, roles that had made them famous.

Yet . . . yet . . . yet . . . as one watched, as one waited, one had the sense that they were mocking themselves, sometimes slowing down, sometimes speeding up, sometimes flagrantly touching in a form of lewd burlesque.

We watched it three times. Tony was silent all through each screening. It was obvious that he was fascinated. It was a form of high-art perversity, if such a thing existed.

"Well?" Tony asked at the end of the third showing.

"I see more each time I watch," I said. "But it means nothing. I can't analyze what I see. I can't tie it to anything real."

"You know," Tony said thoughtfully, "I've never seen him dance except on this tape."

"What do you think of him?"

"He doesn't dance the way I thought he would. I thought he would be more explosive. But maybe that injury was bothering him."

I looked at him, startled. "What do you mean, 'injury'? He looks in fine shape to me."

"I mean the finger, the dislocated finger."

"What are you *talking* about?" I asked in a demanding tone.

Tony shrugged, rewound the tape, and hit the PLAY button. "Look there; look at the last two fingers on his right hand."

I followed Tony's pointing finger. All I saw was what seemed to be a small bandage, around the pinky and the finger next to it.

"When they tie two fingers together like that," Tony explained, "it means that one of them has been dislocated and put back into place. The trainers always tie the two fingers together to keep the dislocated one out of trouble — a kind of support. If the finger was broken they would have splinted it."

"That's not a common injury for dancers, is it?" I asked him.

"I doubt it. More common for basketball or baseball players. And drunks who throw a punch at the wrong guy in a bar."

"Imagine," I was thinking out loud, "if the man who murdered Dobrynin was just another anonymous barroom brawler."

"Crazier things have happened."

I had to follow up on this. I went into the other room and called Melissa Taniment, who was very accommodating now that she'd had time to dwell on the fact that I held the tape. I asked her if she knew anything about the injured finger. She told me that Dobrynin had indeed dislocated a finger just before he'd dropped out of sight three years ago. He had told her that he'd hurt it in a fight in Winnipeg, when he was up there dancing as guest soloist with the Winnipeg Regional Ballet. The finger had never healed properly, Melissa said, but he had refused to seek further medical help.

I hung up and told Tony all that Melissa had said. It was odd how that dislocated little finger was beginning to balloon, resonate. I hadn't noticed the bandage when I saw his body on the balcony. I hadn't spotted it when I viewed the tape for the first time. Why? I suppose it was because I had been too obsessed with my theory about love denied. Now, who was to say what else I had missed?

"You look upset," Tony noted.

"I am."

"What about?"

"Tony," I said, changing the direction of the conversation, "do you know anything about the Winnipeg Regional Ballet?"

"Let's see. I assume it's in Canada."

"Yes, it is, on the Canadian Great Plains. Wheat country. It's practically unique in the ballet world. No one can really explain how this very small, provincial company in a culturally deprived area has produced such talented dancers and choreographers year after year. The company's productions are world-class. But I never knew Dobrynin had danced with them."

"He must have danced with a lot of companies."

"Yes, but he hurt the finger in a fight in Winnipeg."

"So?"

"Tony, the finest dancer in the world doesn't get into brawls. Dobrynin did a lot of crazy things. But dancers go to great lengths to avoid physical confrontations, injuries. Like surgeons. Like racehorses — a tiny bit of pressure exerted the wrong way can break a leg and destroy them."

"But apparently he *did* get into a fight."

"Yes, I'm betting he did. So there must have been something big at stake. Something worth fighting about, taking a risk over. But Dobrynin cared about nothing except self-gratification, right?"

"Well, no. He fed cats."

I picked up one of the felt cat toys and turned it over and over in my hands.

"Tony," I said, "you're going on a little trip."

"Please, Swede. Please have mercy."

"Come now, Tony. Canada's not far. Only a few hours."

"How? By dogsled?"

I pulled out the massive Manhattan white pages, flipping the pages until I had found the reservations listing for Air Canada. I handed the heavy book to Basillio.

"Is this necessary? Is it really bloody necessary?"

I kissed him on the nose. "I have to find out what happened up there," I whispered. "You are supposed to hang in there with me. Remember?"

Tony took both my wrists and slid my arms up his chest and around his neck. He whispered something of his own.

"Oh," said I. "Okay."

19

"Twas a chopt' time," as the poet puts it.

I imagine he meant "choppy" or "ragged." Yes, "ragged" was better. Time seemed ragged as I waited for Tony to return from Canada. For some reason, for some odd reason, I continued to watch that videotape of Melissa and Dobrynin dancing. And when I wasn't looking at that, I was returning to the overstuffed shopping bag in the closet to retrieve and stare at that old photograph in which I appeared as the siren Alice Nestleton, so worldly yet so innocent-looking with that flaxen hair. I looked like some Edwardian incarnation of Baby Doll. I wondered what Dobrynin would have made of me then. Would I have fallen like the numberless others? Lucky I hadn't been in the ballet world. Lucky our paths hadn't crossed. In the intervening years I had come to appreciate just how exquisite male dancers can be.

It was strange that, while I felt I had conducted myself during this case in the most professional of manners, it was only after I had seen the bandage joining two fingers on

Dobrynin's hand that I became fully engaged. Bubbles were beginning to pop into my consciousness.

Visual bubbles, like in the comics. One bubble encircled Betty Ann Ellenville, another Louis Beasley. There was a bubble for each of them. I could see them and then burst them. A bubble for all the rogues and non-rogues. And then a bubble for poor Lucia, awaiting her fate. And, oh yes, a bubble for Mr. Brodsky, the attorney — half-gentleman, half-piranha — sitting among his valuable paintings.

Twenty-four hours had passed. No word from Tony. I'd eaten every Pepperidge Farm cookie in the house — a very bad sign. I often found myself muttering under my breath, "Stay close, Alice. Stay close." It was a phrase my ex-husband had used a lot when I was playing housewife. He'd taken it from his favorite movie, John Ford's *The Searchers*. When John Wayne speaks the words to his younger brother in the film, you know the Duke is alluding to Comanches. I never knew *what* threat my husband was referring to when he spoke them.

But I did stay close. Close to home. I didn't leave the apartment at all. I don't know how long that isolation might have lasted if I hadn't found in a bureau drawer one of those absurdly elongated shoehorns, which someone had given me as a gift many years ago. I stared at it, remembering Louis Beasley's spiel about Dobrynin — how he had used women as shoehorns — and burst out laughing. Not all shoehorns are alike. I went out then to buy some badly needed items.

When I returned, groceries in tow, the phone was ringing. It was Tony. He was at La Guardia. And he was out of cash. Could I meet him downstairs and pay for the cab he was about to take? Yes, of course.

The cab made it from the airport in forty minutes. I rushed down when I heard the horn blasting, paid the driver, and was starting back toward my building when Tony grasped my arm and pointed toward the avenue. "A brandy, Swede. You owe me one."

He was flushed, happy, almost triumphant. We walked to a bar on Second Avenue and I bought the drink for him.

"First let me tell you this, Swede," he said, with growing excitement. "It's not that small a place! It's a city! And it's not all that provincial. There's all kinds of people up there in Winnipeg. Italians and Jews and Indians — American Indians and Indian Indians and West Indians — and Armenians

. . . and God knows who else.

"But, man, is it cold! That wind is something — like in your native land."

So now he was making the logical but crazy jump from calling me "Swede" to referring to Sweden as my "native land." I made a silent vow to say something to Tony about his drinking.

Then he got more serious. He leaned in toward me in one of his poor impersonations of a coconspirator and said, "Very strange happenings up there, Swede. First thing I did was walk into the library and go through back editions of the two biggest newspapers published there, between three and four years ago. And what we were looking for was all over the local papers." He took a long pull on the brandy and looked around the bar, proudly, as if wanting the other patrons to pay homage to his great feat of research. There was, alas, only one other customer at the bar, and he looked far from interested.

Tony smiled at me. "Well, not exactly what we were looking for. But here it is. About three years ago the director of the Winnipeg Ballet, Alexander Luccan, was physically assaulted. He was beaten so bad he had to go to the hospital and stay there for several days. The newspaper stories said that a young dancer in the company had been drinking and had assaulted the director over some grievance — a part he didn't get. Anyway, this dancer wasn't named and no one was charged with the assault.

"The people on the staff at the ballet were decidedly unfriendly when I called on them. And as for Alex Luccan himself, his secretary said he'd be out of town on business for several weeks.

"I did buy lunch for a reporter for one of the papers. He says he was pretty sure at the time that Luccan's assailant was our guy Dobie. But nobody would confirm it."

"So he never put his suspicions into print," I offered.

"Right. And Alexander Luccan decides not to press any charges whatsoever. End of story."

"Was Dobrynin's name ever mentioned?"

"No," Tony said emphatically. "Not in connection with the beating. Only the expected stuff about his appearance with the company. Which you know about from Melissa." He finished his brandy, looked at me with imploring eyes, and then pushed the glass toward the edge of the bar so that the bartender would refill, which he did.

"So, Swede, there you have it. A cover-up. It was probably Dobrynin who gave Luccan that beating, during which he dislocated a finger. But what I don't understand is why they covered it up. I mean, why not say Dobrynin did it? I thought when there's a scandal involving a celebrity that it's good for ticket sales, not to mention newspaper sales."

I didn't respond. The importance of the information that Tony had brought back from Winnipeg was beginning to overwhelm me. His findings had created the possibility of a number of wholly new scenarios. It was now conceivable that the murder of Dobrynin had not necessarily been about his personality or his erotic adventures or his persistent betrayals of those who loved him. It could very well have been about the dancer's place in the world of international ballet — a world of glamour and rivalry and big money and constant deception at all levels. A world that had created the very concept of an international star. A world that has always been marked by financial chicanery — since no ballet company in the history of the world has ever turned a profit.

"Did you hear me, Swede? Why would they cover up?"

I answered him this time. "Alexander Luccan would cover it up if the fight was *not* about alcohol or sexual jealousy or career problems."

"Okay. So what was it about?"

"How about extortion? Or blackmail. Or revenge. Or torture."

"Torture!"

"I mean, if Luccan was beaten because Dobrynin was trying to extract information from him."

"Information about what? This is starting to sound like an espionage plot."

"Oh no, Tony. I don't think it was that simple."

He allowed his head to fall heavily into his hands. "Where do we go from here?" he moaned. "Will you be sending me to Timbuktu — for the waters?"

"Follow the honey to the hive," I said. A strange turn of folksy speech, I realized, but it had just popped out.

"I hope that's your grandmother talking, and not you," Tony said, laughing. "Tell me, where's the honey? And who's the hive?" He found his own question even funnier. "God, now I'm doing it, too!" he chortled. "That misanthropic old bat gets under your skin, doesn't she?"

I raised a fist to him.

"Just kidding, Swede, just kidding."

"What I was trying to say, Tony, is that

the only logical thing to do — the only way to unravel all these knots — is to find the young woman who was paying Lenny to keep quiet."

Tony slammed his palm down on the bar. "Sold!" he said lustily. "Agreed! We follow the money trail; we find the blackmail victim — the blackmailee, I guess; we find the killer. *But how?*"

"A trap," I replied. "Baited with lots of sticky sweet honey." I stood up and paid the bartender.

"Where to now, madame?"

"Not to worry, Basillio. You're not going to Timbuktu. Only as far as the post office on Twenty-third Street."

"*That* I can handle," he said, and gallantly took my arm.

Once inside the bustling post office, I bought three prestamped postcards and carried them over to a counter, to which several cheap ballpoint pens had been chained. One of them actually worked.

I printed the name LOUIS BEASLEY on the front of one card, then his address, then consulted the monstrously big, well-thumbed directory, also riveted to the counter, to obtain his zip code.

The next card I addressed to Betty Ann Ellenville.

The final one was going to Melissa Taniment.

"Okay, Tony," I said, passing the pen on its chain and the postcards over to him. "Your turn now."

"My turn for what?"

"Write exactly what I tell you on the back of each card. You have such a wonderful hand." This was true — Tony has studied calligraphy. I love the bold, beautiful script he writes in.

He waited for my instructions, pen in hand.

"Anna Pavlova Smith," I said.

"Come again? That's what you want me to say?"

"Correct. Write the same thing on the back of all three."

"And that's it?"

"That's it. Want me to spell it for you?"

"No, I can manage the spelling," he said, but he didn't begin to write. He simply looked at me, waiting for my explanation.

"Listen, Basillio. If you had been the victim of Dobrynin's blackmail in the past, and you received a postcard with nothing written on it but 'Anna Pavlova Smith,' how would you react?"

"I'd be confused — because I'd know that

he was dead. And I'd probably be pretty scared as well."

"Um-hum," I said, nodding. "And why would you be so scared?"

"Because I'd thought the threat had vanished. While he was blackmailing me, this was the contact signal he used. Now he's dead. So where's the signal coming from? Somebody else may be planning to pick up where he left off."

"Very good," I said. "You get this card. You're pretty shaken up. What would you do next?"

"I'd probably haul ass over to 1407 Broadway. To check if the old handwriting was on the wall again. Because if it is, I'm in trouble — again."

"Brilliant, Mr. Basillio."

"No, it is you who is brilliant, Miss Nestleton."

"No, *you*, Mr. Basillio."

"No. I insist, Miss Nestleton." Tony gave me a courtly bow. " 'Tis you. In fact," he said admiringly, "you sometimes partake of that soufflé called genius."

20

Tony and I were at the window counter of the twenty-four-hour coffee shop on Seventh Avenue. From where we sat we had an unobstructed view of the downtown face of 1407 Broadway. After nine P.M. the streets began to empty. As the evening wears on, the stretch between the shopping area at Thirty-fourth Street and the wild Forty-second Street entertainment strip becomes just a windy valley quickly traversed by hurrying souls. The colder the night the more quickly they move. And it was a very cold night.

"Are you confident, Swede?" Tony asked, pulling his woolen cap down on his forehead and pouring the usual vast quantities of ugly white sugar into his coffee.

"As long as the mailman didn't let me down," I said, "I'm confident. If they all got those postcards, she's got to show up."

Tony looked around. "Wonder how long they'll let us sit here before they start thinking we're drug dealers."

"I think as long as we keep buying coffee, they won't care who we are."

"But how many more containers can we drink?"

Rather than answer, I simply pointed to the large plastic-lined garbage pail set only a few feet away from us, near the door. Tony nodded his understanding; buy a container, take a few sips, dump the rest.

The chill wind blew in right through the window, but we had dressed for the long, cold haul. In fact it was oddly relaxing to be sitting there, drinking bad coffee, staring at that monolith of a building that occupied the entire city block.

As always, Tony was full of reminiscences: about us . . . then . . . "the old days," as he called them. When we were aspiring . . . arrogant . . . knew what it was all about . . . truth and beauty and Tennessee Williams. I didn't talk much, mostly listened and nodded. Nostalgia is harmless as long as it doesn't determine future actions. As Simone Signoret has said, nostalgia isn't what it used to be.

It was ten-sixteen P.M. — according to the ghastly old fly-specked clock with the Budweiser logo — when we saw a sleek black Lincoln Towncar turn off Broadway onto the downtown side of the street in front of the building. Tony and I were not only awash in coffee but had gone through

190

at least two packets of something called "Yankee Doodles."

We exchanged quick glances, half-frightened, half-anticipatory, ready to move. But the car just kept moving, and soon was out of sight.

But five minutes later it was back.

This time it parked across the street from Basil's writing wall. And it just sat there, idling like a huge, humming bug, its parking lights lit. The windows were of tinted smoke. The payoff car was just as Basil had described it. The white lady, as he'd called her, ought to be sitting in back, waiting.

Basillio and I jumped off our stools. "Just one minute!" He jerked me back. "Exactly what do we do now?"

"Now we flush her out of that car . . . make her commit herself," I said, shaking him off and at the same time withdrawing a new can of spray paint from the pocket of my parka.

"What the hell is that? What are you going to do?"

"Listen carefully, Tony. I'm going to cross to the other side of the street and start writing. You stay back. Play it by ear."

He was confounded. "Play it by . . . Swede, I wonder if you've thought this thing out."

"Thought it out? I'm brilliant, remember? Besides, do you have a better idea?"

He puffed out his cheeks and blew out air slowly, all the while watching the long black car.

Yes, I was frightened. But I was also exhilarated — high as the proverbial kite.

We were out on the pavement by then. I squeezed his arm as I moved off. "Stay close," I cautioned.

I crossed the street rapidly and walked along the building line. The side street was deserted. The wind picked up newspapers, empty cans, all the waste of the day, and blew it around my ankles. I stopped abruptly a few feet from the car, and very deliberately turned to face the wall. Then, with an absurdly grandiloquent gesture I began to write, in letters as large and high as my reach could command.

I had started the second N in ANNA when someone knocked the can from my hand with such force that I fell against the building. Someone was screaming in my ear: "You stupid bitch! What are you doing?" I whirled around and saw a young woman dressed in a ski parka hovering over me.

She had raised her arm as if to strike me. But then I saw another arm — Tony's — enveloping her from behind. The two struggled, and when my heartbeat had slowed a bit I tried to assist Tony in restraining her.

"Stop fighting!" I heard Tony yell at her. "Stay still and you won't get hurt!"

At last, she ceased struggling. But the fight had taken a weird sort of toll on her. There was something grotesque hanging from the left side of her skull. A wig.

I found myself staring into the face of Vol Tcak.

I was trembling so hard I could barely muster the breath to tell Tony who "the white lady" was — not a lady at all, but Louis Beasley's companion.

I heard Basillio tell him: "We're all going to walk calmly over to your car together, like The Three Musketeers, and get into the backseat. Then we'll all go for a short drive."

Vol surprised us both with a very colorful expletive.

"Wow," Tony said. "And I'd heard you weren't too bright."

"I'll go nowhere with you people," Teak reiterated.

I recovered, "Perhaps you'd like me to call Louis Beasley for you."

Fear came into his eyes at the mention of Beasley.

"Perhaps," I continued, "he would be curious about where you got all that money to pay Dobrynin off. He might even be curious as to *why* you were paying him off."

The three of us climbed into the back of the car. I directed the driver uptown.

Frank Brodsky answered the door fully dressed, tasteful as ever. I'd outlined the trap to him earlier in the day, so he'd been waiting up eagerly to hear from us. As he led us into the office, I thought I caught a faint whiff of Scotch on his breath.

In fact there was a cut-glass decanter of what very well might have been Scotch on the table near the club chair where we settled Vol. There was also a pot of coffee, a few other bottles, and a variety of glasses and cups. Tony sat down on the sofa, coat still on, and began to smoke furiously. When it was offered, he hungrily accepted a brandy. I asked for a tonic. Brodsky stood erect near the fireplace. Vol sat with his head in his hands.

We made quite a tableau. A rehearsal for a tried-and-true melodrama? If so, the rehearsal wasn't going very well. For the longest time, no one dared to try out a line.

It was Mr. Brodsky who ultimately broke the silence, using his kindliest voice.

"Mr. . . . Teak, is it? Mr. Teak, you seem to hold the key to a great many questions my colleagues and I have been pondering. I wonder if you'd care to elaborate on tonight's events? We'd all be so grateful."

Vol laughed in a short, staccato burst. Then he stared glumly at the ceiling. The silence returned.

With a great sigh, Brodsky walked over to the high-gloss desk and picked up the receiver of the extension phone that sat there. "Ah, yes," we heard him say. "Will you please give me . . ." He looked over at Vol then. "Whom shall it be first, Mr. Teak? Your friend Mr. Beasley, or one of the police detectives handling the Dobrynin murder?"

Vol moved with deliberation from his chair to the desk. He ripped the receiver from Brodsky's hand and slammed it down loudly in its cradle. I caught only the tail end of the name he called the old attorney, who merely raised an eyebrow.

Then Vol stepped back and shouted to all three of us: "I know who you people are! And I know what you're trying to do! You're trying to implicate me in Peter's murder! You'll do anything to keep Lucia from going to trial! Do you think I'm a fool?"

Frank Brodsky didn't answer right away.

He ambled over to a chair and sat down. "Won't you have a seat, Mr. Teak? Please?"

Vol threw a sullen look at the lawyer, but came back to his chair.

"Now," Brodsky continued, "as you have so perceptively pointed out, we are vitally concerned with preventing Miss Maury's indictment. And while I have no wish to falsely accuse *you* of Mr. Dobrynin's murder, please understand that I mean to know all about this . . . arrangement . . . this partnership you carried on with him."

Vol shivered once, as if he had been touched by some slimy presence, and then his handsome mouth began to spit out words.

"He was blackmailing me."

When Vol halted there, Frank Brodsky shook his head slowly and said, not very patiently, "Yes, yes, Mr. Teak. So we gathered. But I'm afraid that isn't enough. You're going to have to trust the three of us with your secrets. Please be specific."

"Dobrynin was bleeding me," Teak finally went on. "He found out I was getting finder's fees from ballet directors I introduced to Louis. They all need Louis. He's the one they turn to when they need financing. He's gotten seed money for dozens of companies.

"I never got a lot of money from any of them. A few thousand from each one he helped. Louis never knew. No one did, I thought. But somehow that sonuvabitch Dobrynin found out. And he verified it by beating that Canadian director half to death."

"Alex Luccan," Basillio supplied.

"Yes," Teak said bitterly. "He was one of my 'clients.' "

He buried his head in his hands for a moment, then slammed his fist down on the table and exploded: "Dobrynin was a bloodsucker — a monster! He always wanted more . . . always more. He'd always say this one was going to be the last payment, but then he'd come back for more. And the stupid games he played! Like that nonsense of painting Anna Pavlova's name on the building. He had me patrolling that vile neighborhood like a common hooker.

"I started borrowing . . . stealing . . . from Louis. That was the worst part. And when I asked Peter why, why he needed the money — after all, he was living the life of a hobo — he only laughed and said he had to take care of all the lost souls . . . so many forgotten, sick things, he said . . . all the 'lost and hungry ones.'

"And when I threatened to confess everything to Louis, Peter said he'd tell him . . . about us. Something that happened long ago. But he said he'd see that Louis turned me out, prosecuted me for embezzlement. He would have, too. Dobrynin was evil. The cruelest man I've ever known.

"I'm glad he's dead, and I have no apologies to make for feeling that way," Vol said coolly, drawing himself up. "I'm glad! But that doesn't mean I killed him! Because I didn't!"

His outburst had been so pained, so vivid, that it left us all feeling drained.

Then Frank Brodsky broke the silence. "Mr. Teak, why did you need the money you took from those company directors? Those 'fees,' as you euphemistically called them. Isn't your companion a wealthy man?"

Vol now seemed close to breaking down completely. His eyes filled with tears. "Louis has always given me what I've needed. He's hardly the most generous man in the world, but he's taken care of me. I didn't want to use him, though. And I never meant to betray him. I just wanted something of my own. I had to feel . . . independent. I was a dancer, you know. I had two seasons with the Royal."

He looked at the lawyer, as if this characterization of himself as a fine dancer explained everything in the world.

"I suppose, Mr. Teak, that you can account for your whereabouts on the night Peter Dobrynin died?" Brodsky asked mildly.

"I was with a friend," he said quickly.

"Just visiting?"

"I can produce his name if the police demand it!" Vol said defiantly. "But not before."

"I see," Mr. Brodsky said gently, smiling a little. "Well, Mr. Teak, it's been a long night for you. Why don't you go home and get some rest now? I'm sure Mr. Basillio would be happy to see you to your car."

Vol was taken aback by the suddenness with which the interrogation had come to an end. "What are you going to do now?" he asked, obviously frightened.

"Right now, nothing — nothing in reference to you, that is." And he stood and gestured to Tony, who headed over to the door and stood waiting for Teak to join him. We heard their footsteps on the stairs.

When Tony had rejoined us, the attorney asked, "What do you make of it, Miss Nestleton?"

"Vol Teak was tired of paying blackmail to Dobrynin," I said. "He hired Dobrynin's bagman, Basil, to kill him. That's what I make of it."

"And you, Mr. Basillio?"

"She echoes my sentiments exactly."

Brodsky leaned back in his chair, hands clasped together behind his neck. He looked tired. "I agree," he pronounced. "The problem is how to prove it. As you've already told me, Mr. Basil is slippery. He won't confess to any of this willingly."

Brodsky stood suddenly and walked to a small table on the far side of the room. He opened a drawer, extracted a small object, and came back over to us.

I looked at the little white packet that he'd placed on the table in front of me. It was just a small piece of folded paper, its edges tucked in.

"Do you recognize this, Miss Nestleton?"

"No."

He smiled. "This is the kind of wrapper that diamond merchants carry their wares in. This has always intrigued me. One would think they would transport their gems in tiny locked cases, or use all kinds of security devices. But no, they carry them in ordinary white paper envelopes such as this, in their pocket."

He leaned over and unfolded the edges of the packet. Nestled within it were three small cut diamonds.

"Pretty, aren't they?"

Tony and I looked up from the diamonds and at each other, perplexed.

He reclosed the packet, quite happy.

"And now, Miss Nestleton. About that police officer acquaintance of yours — the one who proved helpful in locating the fellow Basil."

"Yes, what about him?"

"Do you think you could call on him to do one more favor?"

"A minor one, I suppose."

"Oh, this would be decidedly minor. And Mr. Basillio, might I ask you for your help?"

"What with?" Tony asked.

"I will need a photograph of Vol Teak. And I will need a small, unobtrusive recording device."

"No problem," Tony said, a bit relieved.

Brodsky nodded. He reached over then and took my hand in a gallant gesture. "I am more than pleased at the way you constructed and sprang your trap for Mr. Teak," he said. "Really. Most admirable."

I nodded silent thanks.

"But," he went on, "I wonder if now I might be allowed to set a trap of my own, with the able assistance — or indulgence — of Mr. Basillio and yourself."

21

It was just a one-act play. The shortest-running one I'd ever appeared in — only one performance. The lead character was a distinguished attorney, shrewd but kindly, aged but sharp-witted — played by Frank Brodsky.

Appearing as the willowy and mysterious lady private investigator — Miss Alice Nestleton.

Her earthy, wise-cracking, jack-of-all-trades sidekick — Anthony Basillio.

And the villain — or the hero, depending on your degree of affection for the rake Peter Dobrynin — that strangely erudite, campily deranged ex-convict known only by the one name, Basil.

Another able player would be making a brief cameo appearance: Detective Rothwax, member in good standing of the NYPD, playing Detective Rothwax, member in good standing of the NYPD.

There was no script, really, although the program should have featured a line stating, "from a concept by Frank Brodsky." And even though the players would be performing without benefit of a director, everyone seemed to know exactly what to do.

It was a kind of sublime exercise in improvisation, made possible by the fact that everyone in it knew exactly how it should end. There was plenty of freedom for us to develop our parts, but we had to take advantage of that freedom quickly, because we knew the play was a short one.

Tony and I opened the first little scene by showing up at Basil's halfway house around twenty minutes before noon. Basil was seated in the television room again, wearing his blue raincoat. He seemed different, more relaxed, as if whatever addictions he was prey to had at least been put on hold. He spoke differently now, too, not by means of that stilted, often cryptic dialogue. He was much more down-to-earth. In fact, when Tony told him we would like to buy him a good lunch with good whiskey accompanying it, Basil smiled and said, "You can do me like that any time. Do me now or do me later." Then he winked at me and asked, "Right, beautiful woman?"

Off the three of us went, to meet the Wizard, who was seated in a back booth in a very upscale eating and drinking establishment on Broadway. I introduced Basil to Mr. Brodsky and we all sat down.

"What shall I call you?" the lawyer asked. "Is it 'Mr. Basil,' or 'Mr. Basil something else'?"

"Call me anything you want. Call me now or call me later," he replied. He was smiling. His eyes roved over the inside of the restaurant. Then a waitress appeared. Tony and I ordered Bloody Mary's. Mr. Brodsky ordered tea. Mr. Basil ordered "rye whiskey."

I saw Tony look at his watch after the drinks had arrived. It was time for the all-important bit player to make his entrance.

And Rothwax arrived on time, just as he had promised.

"What a pleasant surprise!" he boomed out as he approached the table. "You never know who you'll meet in a bar!"

I introduced Detective Rothwax to my companions, saying that he was "one of New York's finest." Tony faked it — pretended he had never met the detective before. Brodsky said that "any friend of Alice Nestleton's is surely a friend of mine."

But Basil said nothing. Rothwax obviously made him uncomfortable — *very* uncomfortable. He sipped at his whiskey slowly, reflectively, staring out over the edge of the glass but not looking at Rothwax at all.

"Won't you join us, Detective?" Brodsky

offered, starting to slide over on the seat to welcome Rothwax.

"Thanks, no," Rothwax declined. "I'm at the bar. I have to leave shortly."

He said good-bye and how nice it had been to bump into me, that he'd enjoyed meeting everyone. Then he returned to the bar. From where we sat, his back was clearly visible. The threat was in place, as planned.

The waitress reappeared. Frank Brodsky ordered an omelet. Tony asked for a small Caesar salad. Basil ordered a turkey sandwich. I wasn't hungry.

The moment our waitress had left, Mr. Brodsky pulled out a photograph and placed it face-up on the center of the table. Basil, who was seated next to the lawyer and across from me, didn't even look at the picture. He kept sipping methodically at his rye.

"Do you know who this man is, Mr. Basil?"

Basil's eyes remained on the photo for only a second. "Don't know him. Don't want to know him."

Frank Brodsky tapped the photograph with his finger. "Pictured here, Mr. Basil, is one Vol Teak. We believe he murdered your friend Lenny because Lenny was blackmailing him. We believe also that he hired you to help him with the murder. Which would be an easy thing to do, given the number of times you came into contact with Mr. Teak. After all, it was you who collected those many envelopes from him, in front of the building at 1407 Broadway."

Brodsky rotated the photograph on the table. "At the very least, you were the one who managed to get into an office at Lincoln Center and secrete a gun beneath a desk there. So now, Mr. Basil, you are going to be given a chance to save your skin. I assure you that if you tell us all you know, things will go a lot easier for you with the police. They want the murderer, not the messenger. Of course, if you yourself pulled the trigger . . . well, that's another matter altogether. But we don't think you did. We believe you to be an innocent victim of an evil man."

The old lawyer actually patted Basil's arm before adding: "And I think you are very sorry about the part you played in Lenny's death. I really believe you didn't understand what Vol Teak was going to do. After all, Mr. Basil, judging from appearances, you seem to be a righteous man."

We waited. Basil continued to nurse his rye. At last he looked over in silent condemnation of me for having set him up. His eyes traveled slowly over to the bar area, and then back to me.

"Don't know the man," Basil said icily. "Don't know you. Don't know the beautiful Judas."

With a sigh, Mr. Brodsky picked up the photo and returned it to his pocket.

The food arrived then. The rest of my party ate slowly, in silence. Basil made no move to go but ate his sandwich fastidiously, albeit with great dispatch. He kept glancing at the bar, where Rothwax was so clearly visible — a threat without being threatening.

Then Brodsky made a deal out of accidentally dropping his fork. When he'd been given a new one, he turned to Basil again and said, "My memory seems to be failing me these days, Mr. Basil. There was one other question I had meant to ask you. A very important question."

Basil chewed the last bit of his sandwich, not looking at Brodsky.

"My question is," the attorney went on, "have you ever heard of a man by the name of Kurt van Holsema?"

Still not meeting Brodsky's look, Basil just shook his head, angry but restrained.

"Well, sir," Brodsky said, that hint of steel beginning to infuse his voice, "I think you *do* know him. But perhaps not by name. Mr. van Holsema is a Dutch businessman who now lies in Lenox Hill Hospital. His business is diamonds. And a few days ago he was mugged — knifed — after leaving a concert at Lincoln Center. Of course the culprit stole his watch and wallet, credit cards, and things of that nature. But something much more precious than that was taken. A packet of diamonds he was carrying. The man who robbed and stabbed him, Mr. Basil, bore an uncanny resemblance to yourself."

Basil looked up then.

"Yes, isn't it an amazing coincidence?" Brodsky said. "He even wore the same sort of coat as you do, and he too has a thin mustache."

Tony and I stared at each other. Basil gazed down at his now empty plate.

Brodsky moved in for the kill. "Would you do me a favor, Basil? Would you be good enough to reach into your left coat pocket and remove what you find there?"

Basil's hand went quickly to the pocket. It grasped at something and then pulled it out.

Mr. Brodsky said, "Now put that item on the table, would you please . . . ? Good. Now if you would be so kind, please open it. Yes . . . splendid."

For a few moments we all sat gazing at the

sparkling gems as they caught the light.

"You see, Mr. Basil, this packet of diamonds, which has been in your possession, is the one stolen from the poor Dutch gentleman. Why, I saw you remove them from your pocket with my own eyes. And I daresay one wouldn't be at all surprised to find various other items rightly belonging to Mr. van Holsema, say, in the place where you reside?"

"Ain't no such thing happened to no Dutchman!" Basil said, seething. "You *know* it ain't, Nellie!"

"Ah," Brodsky said sagely. "But there is a Dutchman who will say it did. As will I. Now, doesn't that amount to the same thing?"

Basil's head twisted wildly toward the bar then. Rothwax was there, solid as ever, but this time he was looking dead into Basil's eyes.

"Let me explain something to you, Basil," the attorney said. "I'll explain it very carefully, because I don't want you to have any questions left in your mind. If you describe to us the circumstances that caused you to go to work for Vol Teak, you will serve, at most, a year in prison. I will personally involve myself in your case. This assumes, however, that you didn't pull the trigger yourself. Now, as you must realize, if you are arrested for the diamond theft and assault — and believe me, you will be — you may never see the light of day again. That's how deep you'll be buried in the state prison system."

Basil looked back down at his plate. I thought his face might literally crack. This was the most effective scam I had ever seen or participated in — and the cruelest. It was ugly beyond belief. I knew there was no diamond merchant, no stolen watch, or any of those other things. I knew that Brodsky had simply slipped the diamonds into Basil's pocket. I knew that he was brilliantly playing to the eternal paranoia of the street criminal. Did Basil believe he had knifed the merchant? It didn't matter. He knew what the police would believe. I felt a sudden dreadful shame at playing even a minor role in this whole theatrical piece.

But what if it worked? What if Basil knew a great deal, and would now be willing to talk? *Then* would the end have justified the means? I found I was unable to look at Mr. Brodsky. He knew I wouldn't interfere. He knew that if push came to shove, I would trade Basil for Lucia. He knew that I would hurt Basil if that hurt would save Lucia. He knew it. I knew it. Everyone knew it.

Basil said, "He paid me."

"Who paid you?" Brodsky asked, in a tone that sounded almost bored.

"The man."

"By that do you mean Vol Teak? The man in the photograph I showed you?"

"Him."

"What did he pay you for?"

"To take Lenny into Lincoln Center on Christmas Eve."

"And did you do as he asked?"

"Yeah. Christmas Eve. I took him there and left him. He was drunk. We both were. I stole some newspapers and made out we were trying to sell early editions. We went in through the parking garage. I gave the man there twenty bills. I left Lenny there."

"How much did Teak pay you?"

"A hundred bills."

"Did you know he meant to kill Lenny?"

"Never figured it. No way. Never figured any of it."

"Did you supply Teak with the .25-caliber weapon that killed Lenny?"

"No. I told him a while ago where to get guns. There's this guy works at a hardware store, on Columbus. That's all I told him."

"Did you go into an office and plant a gun there — under a desk?"

"Never *saw* any gun, I said. All I did was

get Lenny there. And I left him there. Alive."

"Thank you so much, Mr. Basil," Brodsky said. He removed a small tape recorder from somewhere under the lip of the table, almost in slow motion. This was the old man's moment of triumph. He had cleared his client.

Then he picked up the diamonds, still nestled in the folded paper, and dropped them one by one into what was left of my Bloody Mary. He smiled broadly. "Fakes," he noted.

22

All charges were dropped against Lucia Maury. The DA's office began to assemble a case against Vol Teak and Basil, whose real name turned out to be Charles Small and who had a long prison record. The combination of Basil's confession and the revelation of Teak's financial relationship with Dobrynin constituted a powerful prima facie case.

There was only one weak link, and that was the gun. Basil had confirmed to the police what he'd told Brodsky — that all he knew about the weapon was that it had probably been obtained by Teak from an illegal gun dealer he, Basil, had recommended. That person, no longer an employee at the hardware store he'd mentioned, could not be located, and Basil's memory of what he looked like was vague.

But the DA's office was confident. I had supplied them with a statement describing my Anna Pavlova Smith trap and recounting, to the best of my ability, Teak's confession of how he had obtained money from various ballet company officials in exchange for his help in getting Louis Beasley's endorsement of them. And of course I told them about Dobrynin's blackmail scheme.

Given all this, no wonder Lucia and her attorney were holding what could only be described as a victory party in her apartment that brutally cold Sunday afternoon. Tony had decided not to accompany me, on the grounds that, one, he had had his fill of ballet folks, and two, he really no longer liked Frank Brodsky. So I went unescorted.

The apartment was already crowded when I arrived. There were large quantities of hastily obtained food and drink. It looked as if dozens of small neighborhood stores had been contacted at the last moment, for the buzzer kept ringing as delivery boys brought up new packages of edibles. There was Italian food, there was Jewish delicatessen, there were savory Indian and Mexican treats.

Lucia looked tired but happy, and she embraced me with such fervor and determination that she nearly choked me. Her aged parents, who had come up from Delaware, thanked me profusely for all my efforts in Lucia's behalf. There were warm embraces and tears all around.

I disengaged myself from the Maury

family and went over to one of the tables laden with food. I spread a tantalizing dip on a strange-looking little cracker. Just as I was about to bite into the canapé I saw Frank Brodsky, alone on the sofa with a martini in hand, looking at me. I put the cracker down and smiled pleasantly at him. He returned the smile and lowered his head in a courtly little nod. I turned away from the food table then and started across the room to join a group of Lucia's dancer friends I hadn't seen in years.

"Alice Nestleton! Hello, Alice!" I heard my name being called above the din. I saw a woman waving at me a bit wildly. It was the dance critic Betty Ann Ellenville. She started to wave me toward her. I allowed myself to be reeled in. When I reached her she grabbed my arm and asked: "Can we go somewhere to talk? Maybe into the bedroom?"

"Sure," I said, and allowed myself to be guided into the bedroom, where coats and scarves and sweaters seemed to cover every surface.

"It's a little too noisy to talk out there," Betty Ann said apologetically.

"Have you been here long?"

"For weeks, it feels like. But I'm not complaining. It's nice to see so many old acquaintances, and to see Lucia on her feet again. In fact, it sort of reminds me of the party scene in *Laura*. I've always loved that film. But listen, Alice, I have a great favor to ask of you. A pretty big one."

"I'll do my best."

She squeezed my arm then. "I had a long conversation the other day with Melissa Taniment."

"Oh, really?"

"Yes. We've been in touch lately, because I've finally decided to write the book I've always wanted to write — about the life and times of Peter Dobrynin. Melissa's not only agreed to cooperate and tell me about her part in his life, but she's giving me a great deal of important information about Peter when he was a very young dancer, about his first roles, about how they fell in love . . . oh, lots of things." She paused, looking rather sheepish, and then said: "Melissa told me about Peter's secret apartment. And about the tape you found."

"You can tell her to relax. I destroyed the tape just the other day."

"Melissa suggested that I go over to the apartment. She says she thinks I might be able to find some notes and scores that could be very helpful to me in doing the book."

"Are you sure that's all she suggested you look for?" I asked cynically.

Betty Ellen laughed. "Well, no. She was quite honest with me. She told me about the long, crippling affair she's had with Dobrynin these last few years. She says she's still fearful there are other things in the place that might possibly compromise her. She asked me, if I go there, to destroy anything like that, so her husband never finds out. I agreed, of course. She suggested that I ask you to take me over there."

There was an awkward silence. It was the kind of request I hadn't anticipated anyone making. The case was closed. The videotape had been destroyed. That's all, folks. But I liked Betty Ann, and she had been helpful to me when I needed information.

"All right. I'll take you there," I said. "Just call me at home when —"

She interrupted. "I thought maybe, since this party's so noisy and the food is so bad, maybe we could go there now."

"Now?"

"Yes! We can get a cab and just go!" she replied enthusiastically, as if she were going off to plunder the riches of some historical treasure house.

Her enthusiasm was catching. "Why not?" was all I could think to say. We began searching for our coats.

The moment the taxi had dropped us in front of the building on West One Hundred and Twenty-sixth Street, I knew something was wrong. There was a huge dumpster out in front, filled to the brim with the residue of either construction or deconstruction: pipes, sheets of soiled fiberglass, ruined carpeting, broken wood. We went into the lobby. It was filled with stacks of paneling that had been ripped from the walls. There were puddles of water and shards of glass all over the floor.

"We came just in time, I think," said Betty Ann, looking around bewilderedly. "The building may not be here tomorrow."

I called out, "Hello! Hello!" But there was no answer. There seemed to be no one in the building — neither tenants nor workers nor the superintendent, whose name I couldn't recall, who had let Tony and me into the apartment. But all the doors were open. It would be easy to get into Dobrynin's place.

We inched along the wall and up the stairs. Footing was difficult and slippery. All heating seemed to have been turned off, and there were cold drafts whistling through the building. I stopped once during the ascent and asked Betty Ann, "Are you sure you want to do this?"

"Yes, yes! Go ahead."

We reached Peter Dobrynin's hideaway. Not only was it open, but the steel entry door had been completely removed. What a mess we found inside! The ceiling had been ripped out, as had most of the plumbing. The glass mirror was still there, but the practice barre had been dismantled.

In the center of the large room was a tarpaulin, and onto it the wreckers had dumped all of Dobrynin's possessions — records, clothing, posters, everything.

We approached the pile. The objects were thoroughly soaked from dripping water. If there was anything of value in the pile, it was so no longer. All of it had turned into a large glob, particularly anything made of paper.

Betty Ann stared morosely at the mess. Her descent from joy to misery had been a swift one. She took my arm and we wandered about the ruined space, looking for something, anything that might have been left unspoiled. We peered into the small bathroom. The sink was still intact, but all the floor tiles had been removed.

We reached the small galley kitchen. "Well," Betty Ann noted wryly, "at least Melissa doesn't have to worry about anything incriminating being found in *here!*"

The stove had been disconnected, the gas obviously having been shut off. The wall behind the kitchen had been broken through, and it was obvious that the renovation included the removal of all walls on the lower floors.

Only the small refrigerator was functioning. I realized why as soon as I opened it — the workmen were keeping their six-packs in there. The top of the refrigerator was covered in candy wrappers.

"What's that?" Betty Ann asked, pointing to a small shelf about three feet over the refrigerator. I was just tall enough to reach the three old-fashioned cookie jars that had been miraculously spared from the devastation.

One jar was empty. The second held twistums and a few small pencils. The third jar contained some stale candy.

I brought the last jar down and shook a few of the candies into my palm. "I guess Dobrynin liked M & Ms," I said, displaying the candy to Betty Ann.

She stared closely at the little candy pieces. "Alice," she said at last, "those aren't M & Ms."

She plucked one of the tablets out of my hand and held it close to one of the wall lights.

"What are they, then?"

"Medicine," she said. "Haldol. A stabilizing medicine for psychotics. And a very heavy-duty one, at that. They use it in mental hospitals. My mother was on Haldol for many years."

I took one of the pills and twirled it between my fingers. Betty Ann had spoken with authority about the medicine, and I believed her. As I looked closer at the tiny print on the tablet, I could see that it did not say "M & M."

"Was Peter in a mental hospital, Alice?"

"Not that I know of."

"How else can you explain these?"

"Maybe they're Basil's."

"Who?"

"The black man who implicated Vol Teak in Peter's death. Basil stayed here sometimes, from what I gathered."

She didn't seem to be listening to me. She had started to pace, agitated, playing with a handful of the pills.

"Why has this upset you so?" I asked. "What does it matter if Dobrynin was in a mental hospital? We know who killed him now, and why. And it had nothing to do with anyone's mental health."

She made a disparaging gesture with her hand, as if I just didn't understand the situation. "Don't you see, Alice? How can one write a true history of Peter Dobrynin if one doesn't even know whether he was clinically insane? How can you understand his genius if you don't understand the source of it?"

It was much too cold and wet to stay there listening to Betty Ann's intellectual problems. I agreed that it was an important thing to know, I even promised to help her find out. But first I wanted to get both of us out of that creepy building.

The next morning, Monday, I called Rothwax and asked the detective for yet another favor. I was becoming a nuisance to him, but for some odd reason he didn't even protest this time. He didn't even engage in any of his usual banter. Maybe being assigned to OC cases had affected his personality. He promised to get back to me in a few hours.

In fact, I heard from him in less than two. He told me that according to the computer there had been no hospital admissions of any kind for either Peter Dobrynin or Charles Small (Basil's real name) in the state of New York over the past three years.

I relayed that information to Betty Ann by phone. She was unhappy to receive it. "You don't understand, Alice. No one just *pre-*

scribes Haldol. It's a major anti-psychotic drug. It's used in hospitals alone, or in the out-patient clinics connected to them." I took a few minutes to sympathize with the problem all this posed for the biography, but there was nothing further that I could do.

Tuesday was a warmish day. Tony and I decided to have our own victory celebration. After all, while it was Brodsky who had put the final nail in Teak's coffin by cagily obtaining Basil's confession, it was Tony and I who had uncovered the extortion that had opened up the whole case and led inexorably to the dropping of all charges against Lucia. Yes, we deserved a celebration, too, and we financed it with the leftover money from the expense account Brodsky had set up for us.

We got into our winter finery and lunched at the Plaza. Then we took in a movie. Then on to Bloomingdale's, where each of us purchased something frivolous — Tony an expensive sweatshirt, and I a very long scarf made in India. We had coffee and brandy at The Sign of the Dove. Then we went back to the Pickwick Arms, to Tony's room, and made love.

When I finally stole a glance at the clock it

was seven in the evening, and I knew it was time to get back to my apartment. I had all kinds of work to catch up on at home. But it really had been a wonderful day, and I simply didn't feel like leaving yet. Tony was still lying naked on the bed. As I sat in the easy chair I told Tony for the first time all about the Haldol we had found, and about Betty Ann's belief that Dobrynin had been hospitalized. I also told him that Rothwax had run a check and found no admission for Dobrynin.

"Betty Ann's writing a book about Dobrynin, so she's anxious to find out just how disturbed he was."

"She'd have to go a long way to find someone as crazy," Tony judged.

"Well, she's talking about the clinical kind of craziness."

"You mean she wants to see it in black and white that someone in a hospital wrote down that he was a paranoid schizo, or whatever?"

"Yes, I suppose it's something like that. If she's going to write a book about the successor to Nijinsky, she'll have to have insanity in the plot."

"I hope there'll also be some *humor* in the plot."

"Was there anything funny about Peter Dobrynin?"

"What, are you kidding? I mean, when you get right down to it, that vaudeville team of derelicts — Lenny and Basil — was pretty damn funny. Here they go — feeding stray cats chicken Kiev. There they go — getting ready to dance *Giselle* in the nude. Come on, Swede, face facts. If someone was going to make a movie about that duo it would be a comedy, and Robin Williams would play Lenny. Richard Pryor would be Basil."

I found his comments oddly disquieting. No, I had never thought that Dobrynin and his companion were funny. Not at all. How strange that Tony should envisage them as a vaudeville team — Lenny and Basil.

"Did I say something wrong?" Basillio asked, suddenly concerned that he might have irritated me or dissipated the glow that still hung in the air between us.

"Not at all, Tony. You're making me think. It's just so odd thinking of them as a vaudeville team."

"Well, they did use stage names, didn't they? We know 'Lenny' isn't Dobrynin's name. And Basil's real name is Charlie Small. Right?"

It was absurd but true. After all, Dobrynin had been in the theater — why *wouldn't* he have selected a stage name? But stage names often have some kind of personal or professional significance. Lenny and Basil . . . Basil and Lenny. The two names were linked somehow . . . weren't they?

"Tony, don't you think that if Dobrynin chose those names they must have some meaning — some relation to ballet?"

"I would imagine."

Lenny and Basil. Basil and Lenny. I crunched them in my mind, trying to fit them into every ballet I could think of. No, that wasn't it. Lenny and Basil weren't characters in a ballet.

Suddenly the origin of those names became so clear to me that I burst out laughing.

"What the hell is the matter with you, Swede?"

"I know what the names mean now, Tony! I know what they stand for! It's so simple, it's almost unbelievable."

"Well, tell me!"

"Did you ever hear of the Ballet Russe de Monte Carlo?"

"Vaguely. I think it's mentioned in *The Red Shoes.*"

"It was the most famous company in the world for almost half a century. The last great impresario of the company was a man named De Basil. And the last great dancer-choreographer of the company was Leonid Massine — Lenny, for short."

"Basil and Lenny," Tony said. "Well, it fits."

"How stupid of me not to have picked up on that. It couldn't be anything else."

"I think I know a way to doublecheck it," he said.

"How?"

"If old Dobie was in fact a mental patient, I'll bet he used the full stage name as a pseudonym: Leonid Massine. Check hospital records under that name."

"Sometimes, Tony, you're a very smart man." I kissed him on top of his head and took a cab home.

23

I really don't know why I asked Rothwax the very next morning to run yet another computer search on Dobrynin — this time under the name of Leonid Massine. I mean, there was no rush. What did it really matter if he'd used that name? Perhaps I was just curious if my theory as to the origin of the stage names, and Tony's as to the hospital admission, were correct. Or perhaps I really felt obliged to help Betty Ann. Or perhaps I couldn't let Dobrynin alone. Who knows? But I made the call, and the information that Rothwax provided was unsettling.

A Leonid Massine had indeed been admitted to St. John's Psychiatric Hospital, in Smithtown, Long Island, seven times during the past three years. Seven times!

The minute I discovered that, I picked up the phone to call Betty Ann Ellenville and give her the news. But then I hung the phone up as quickly as I had picked it up. Why tell her anything yet? Why not first find out how much more I could learn?

One thing was certain: I was going to go out there. I wanted to *know*. I wanted to play this thing out to the very end. So I called Tony and told him the news, then asked him to rent a car and drive me out to Smithtown.

He resisted at first. He didn't understand why I wanted to go out. What did it matter if Dobrynin had been psychotic or not? He was dead. His murderer had been caught. What was the point?

"Humor me, Tony," was all I could say. He hemmed, he hawed, he pleaded, he cursed. Then he rented the car.

As mental hospitals go, St. John's Psychiatric was a breath of fresh air. It was large, freshly painted, rambling, and busy. Patients, relatives, and health-care workers choked the lobby. There was a coffee shop, a newsstand, a cafeteria. There were dozens of bulletin boards scattered everywhere, chockful of notices announcing AA meetings, GA meetings, meetings and parties and prayer meetings of all kinds.

But when we tried to get to see the physician who had treated Dobrynin, we ran into a stone wall of nurses and administrators. They shuffled us back and forth, suspicious, constantly reiterating that patients have rights, and that the hospital could release no information on them unless presented with a valid court order.

"Why are we here? Why are we doing this? Who cares?" Tony kept muttering in my ear.

Finally I turned on him in a fury. "Because when everything is said and done and Vol Teak has been convicted of murder, and when all the damn t's have been crossed and the i's dotted, we still won't know a damn thing about Peter Dobrynin! So let's find out *one* real thing before we close the case! *Okay,* Tony?"

My outburst quieted him. We kept on pushing, begging, moving from office to office until finally one administrator relented and sent us to Dr. Arnold Newmark, whose office was deep inside one of the locked wings.

He was a small, kindly-looking man with gray hair. He wore a white clinician's coat over shirt and tie, and in his pocket were what appeared to be dozens of pens and a large spiral pad.

"Please sit down," he said. "I understand you are looking for information on one of my patients. And I am sure you realize that there is very little I can tell you, legally."

We sat, thankfully. I then lied to him outrageously. I said that Tony and I were private investigators, hired by Leonid

Massine's family. Massine had been reported missing three months ago. The police had failed to turn up any leads. All we wanted was some kind of information — any kind — that would help us in our search for this sad man.

It seemed Dr. Newmark was unable to withstand this solicitation of his kindness. "I'll tell you what I can," he said.

"Well," I said, "I think the first thing you can tell us is why Mr. Massine ended up in a mental hospital."

Dr. Newmark folded his hands on his desk. "Mr. Massine is a bipolar manic-depressive. And he rapid-cycles, which means simply that he moves between mania and depression with great speed and frequency. This disorder is treatable with lithium and antidepressants. The lithium keeps the individual from going through the ceiling, and the antidepressants keep him from going through the floor. But in Mr. Massine's case, such treatment hasn't worked. In fact, in about twenty percent of clinical cases of bipolar manic-depression, such treatment doesn't work."

Tony jumped in. "But I thought manic-depression was common. Most people who have it aren't in mental hospitals, right?"

Dr. Newmark nodded. "Each time Mr.

Massine admitted himself to this hospital he was experiencing a severe manic episode, during which he was dangerous both to himself and to others. In addition, he was exhibiting severe delusional thinking. Mr. Massine is a difficult patient. He is often in the quiet room." When Dr. Newmark saw the stricken expression that came over my face at the mention of a "quiet" room, he explained: "It's a more humane way of restraining violent patients — just an empty padded room."

"His family told us that he was given Haldol," I noted.

"Yes. The delusions generally vanish when the manic high wears off. In his case, the delusions persist. Haldol is indicated."

"What *were* these delusions?"

"Quite strange — and very persistent." He paused and held up his hand, as if he had remembered something important. "You know, I think I've saved something very interesting . . . a drawing Mr. Massine made for me." Dr. Newmark left the desk and wandered over to his file cabinets. He opened and closed drawers, shuffled folders, and finally emerged with one large piece of white sketching paper.

"Look," he said, handing me the paper.

I held the drawing and stared at it.

The blood seemed to drain out of my face. My whole body suddenly became weak. My fingers had trouble holding on to the paper.

The drawing obviously had been made by a psychotic individual. But even with the bizarre strokes, I knew I was looking at a drawing of a large and very malevolent tom.

I sensed Tony coming over, staring at the drawing over my shoulder. I heard him say to Dr. Newmark, "A cat? Was that his delusion — a cat?"

"Well," the doctor replied, "that is part of his delusion, a large part. Mr. Massine seems to think that he is being stalked by a monstrous cat that is hunting him to exact vengeance on him. For what, he never states. But it seems the vengeance will be in the form of genital mutilation."

"Ouch," Tony mumbled. He removed the drawing from my hands and gave it back to Dr. Newmark, who then noted: "This delusional assailant of Mr. Massine's also has a name, a very bizarre name. But I can't recall it."

I was frightened to say the name, but I knew it. Yes, I knew the name. I closed my eyes, and saw it written in red on the hearse in front of the church. "Anna Pavlova Smith," I said quietly.

"Yes. How did you know?" Dr. Newmark asked. "I always found it a strange name for any cat, but particularly a male one."

As we left, Dr. Newmark said: "You know, the name Leonid Massine always seems to jog my memory somehow. Why is it so familiar?"

He didn't receive a reply

Tony took my arm when we reached the nurse's station. "What's the matter with you, Swede? You look like you've seen a ghost."

I found it hard to speak, hard to walk, to think. It had all fallen apart — all my work.

"We have made a terrible mistake, Tony. Vol Teak did not murder Peter Dobrynin." And that was all I could say.

Tony stayed with me at my apartment that night. But it was a sleepless, agitated, loveless night for me. I finally left the bed at around four-thirty in the morning and fixed some coffee. I brought a cup into the living room and lay on the floor with the exiled Bushy.

Tony joined us in the living room just as it was growing light. He sat down beside me and said, "You're working yourself into a frenzy over nothing, Swede. Believe me, nothing we learned out there at the hospital has any bearing on the real world."

I managed to smile at him. "Dobrynin's delusion, Tony, *was* his real world."

"What does that mean?"

"We'll both find out soon, I hope. But let me explain to you where I went wrong — where we all went wrong. The whole logic of the investigation was wrong. We concentrated on the symptoms rather than the cause. We concentrated on Dobrynin's derelict years, the last three years of his life, when we should have been concentrating on the time period before he became Lenny the derelict. Do you understand what I'm saying, Tony? We messed up a good script. We put the wrong costumes on the wrong players."

"I told you you have an academic bent, Swede. I don't understand a word of what you just said. Forget all this 'logic of the investigation' garbage. Just tell me what's going on with you! Did we all make a mistake? Okay, we did. Then who killed Dobrynin?"

It was best, I realized, to keep my own counsel, for what I was thinking at that moment was very strange . . . quite unbelievable. It was best just to proceed . . . to say nothing . . . to do what had to be done. I felt that I had to be careful. That no one could be trusted; even, oddly, myself.

"Tony, I need your help. Think back on what you know of Dobrynin, what we learned about him from our research. I'm talking about when he was still dancing, before he dropped out and into his crazy world. What would you say characterized his life?"

"Women — sex."

"Besides that."

"Booze."

"Would you say he was an alcoholic?"

"If he wasn't, no one is. He seemed to spend all his time in bars or cafés or at parties. He probably drank himself into his psychosis. But you know what they say about Russians and booze."

"He was only half-Russian. But as regards his drinking, I agree with you. Now tell me, don't most alcoholics have their favorite bars?"

"Sure."

"What were Dobrynin's favorite bars? Who are the bartenders who knew him? Who let him drink when he was temporarily out of cash? Who listened to him talk? Who heard his pre-psychotic musings?"

"In other words, you're going bar-hopping."

"But to which bars, Tony? How will I find them?"

"All those gossip columns, I guess. Go back and look at them again. You know how they do it: So-and-so was seen with so-and-so at such-and-such trendy new bistro."

Yes, that was the way to go. But still my thoughts were spiraling wildly. *Anna Pavlova. Anna Pavlova Smith. Cat. Nude tapes.* Checking back through old celebrity-peeping columns in the daily papers might be the perfect, mundane antidote for a disordered state of mind.

"Help me on this one, Tony!" I said desperately.

"On *what?* Help you on *what?*" Tony demanded loudly. "I don't know what you're getting at. You look like *you* belong in that hospital now." He bounded out of his chair. "All right, all right! Sure. I'm in this with you to the bitter end. But once you get in these crazy cat moods, nothing ever —" He stopped in his tracks, looked at me, and laughed wildly. "It was Anna Pavlova Smith who murdered Dobrynin! Right?"

"In a way, Tony," I said calmly.

He raised his eyes reverently to the ceiling and brought his hands together in a prayerful gesture.

We spent three days in the library going over the microfiche, viewing hundreds of gossip and "about town" columns in newspapers and magazines.

Tony worked as hard as I did, but he kept muttering and complaining and sometimes outright taunting me. He kept saying, "Come on, Sweet Alice, tell me what you have. Tell me what that stupid cat drawing really meant. Tell me all about the mysterious Anna Pavlova Smith. If you have something, share it with your partner."

I told him nothing. It was all too inchoate, at that point. It was a bunch of little things that were slowly falling into place in my head. Dobrynin feeding stray cats . . . Dobrynin thinking a cat was hunting him with a view toward emasculation . . . Dobrynin's infatuation with that name, Anna Pavlova Smith. Oh, there were so many things. Things Tony wouldn't understand. He would just think my lifelong obsession with cats was dovetailing nicely with Dobrynin's psychotic delusion about one nonexistent monster cat. No, it was best to keep my mouth shut.

At the end of the three days we consolidated our notes. Going over them together, we noted that there were really only two kinds of references to the dancer in the columns. Two genres of gossip. The first had to do with Dobrynin the bad boy, as he

238

played out his assigned role of enfant terrible of the ballet world. These always
seemed to mention well-known Manhattan
bars and night spots such as P.J. Clark, or
the Algonquin, or a host of whimsically
named Soho and Tribeca bars.

The other type simply noted that the
dancer had been seen in such-and-such a
place with such-and-such companion. That
was all.

What was very interesting about the two
types of references was that in the second
sort Dobrynin was always in a totally different kind of place than he was in the first.
Which is to say, places like the piano bar of
the Hotel Carlyle, the Polo Bar of the West-
bury, or a whole host of small, elegant cafés
that radiate out from Madison Avenue in
the Sixties and Seventies and are the
stomping ground of the quietly rich East
Side denizen, the older European tourist,
and very old New York money.

It was as if he had divided his drinking life
into two distinct parts, one wild and one
sedate.

"So what?" Tony asked, after we'd discovered the pattern.

"So, Tony, you and I are going to produce and star in a little costume drama.
We'll dress up and spend some time in some

of those genteel *boites* where the rich get soused."

"But why?"

"Simple. I want to find a confidant of Dobrynin. Maybe a kindly old-world bartender who fed him drinks and tapas — and listened to him."

"Fine. And what is Dobrynin supposed to have told this confidant — that he secretly wanted a career as a cat portraitist?"

"No, dear. He told him the murderous secret of Anna Pavlova Smith."

If we were going to move, even briefly, among Manhattan's quiet rich, Tony and I would have to create roles for ourselves. And I dreamed up two of them so delicious that even Tony, appalled at the fact that I was continuing the case, found them amusing.

He and I would be husband and wife, in from Spokane, Washington, for our yearly visit to the Big Apple. We — especially I — were balletomanes, and the principal reason for our visit was to see the various dance companies perform and to soak up the sheer excitement of the ballet milieu. Toward that end, we were stopping in at several bars that the great Peter Dobrynin was said to have frequented. I was on a sort of arcane pilgrimage, following in the steps of the master.

As for clothes, it would be necessary to appear wealthy but blasé, to have it be obvious, yet not blatant, that we had money up the nose. Hence I decked myself out in the colors and shapes and hemlines and accessories *Women's Wear Daily* and *W* and *Vogue* told me were appropriate.

Most of our targeted cafés open at around four in the afternoon, but a few of them do have a lunch trade. Banquo, for instance. Though no one was about when we arrived.

It was pretty dark inside, but the gloom was pierced by the brightly polished deep-dark wood, the silver, and the glasses. No plastic here. The bar itself was tiny. Then there was a cocktail table area. And toward the rear, larger dining tables.

Polishing glasses behind the bar was a Filipino wearing one of those cutaway outfits one might have seen in England a hundred years ago. He was a youngish man with strong-looking hands, and he polished with an almost gleeful commitment.

The moment he saw us approach he flew into action, placing in front of each of us two napkins. Yes, two napkins apiece. The first was a square paper napkin with the name BANQUO printed on both sides. The second was a large, folded linen napkin.

Tony picked up the cloth one, grinned, and whispered to me, "The rich must drool a lot."

We ordered drinks, wincing as the register toted up sixteen dollars.

The bartender went back to his polishing. It was time for me to start acting. "Excuse me!" I called out to him in a breathy voice. He looked up and moved closer to us, ever-obliging. "This may seem silly to you," I said self-deprecatingly, "but I've heard that this is one of the places Peter Dobrynin, the dancer, used to frequent. We were great fans of his, my husband and I — we're from Spokane, you know, up in Washington State? — and, like I said, we were just tremendous fans. . . . Oh, I know I'm acting like a schoolgirl with a crush, but . . . well . . . did he really come here all the time? Like they used to say in the papers?"

A look of pain creased the bartender's brow. For the first time, it occurred to me that his English might not be the best. After a moment's thought he said, "Peter who?"

So went our first excursion.

But I could hardly retire a character like that after just one matinee. So we went to two other posh little places. In both the bartenders recognized the name of the great dancer, and one said he had heard that Dobrynin used to come in occasionally, but that had been before he was hired.

Tony and I spent the next few hours relaxing at the Frick Museum. At four-thirty we headed for another café that had been mentioned many times in the columns — Camilla's.

The place was still there, but it was no longer called Camilla's. The name on the canopy was VINE. Like the others it was intimate, gleaming, ordered. The bar was a bit larger, and very high off the ground, I thought. Behind it stood an elderly man in formal jacket who looked very much like T. S. Eliot.

Prissy, he was, but approachable. If not Eliot, then Clifton Webb. Tony said he thought Franklin Pangborn was the model, but I disagreed with that.

Incredibly, the man bowed as Tony and I seated ourselves on the uncomfortably tall stools. Off liquor for the rest of the day, we asked for club sodas with lime. He smiled at the order, as if to say that it was a brilliant choice, then made a great fuss about preparing the drinks and setting them out in front of us. He capped his performance with another bow.

As he presented to us a silver bowl filled with mixed nuts, I immediately went into my starry-eyed dance-fan routine.

At the end of it, he reached across the bar and patted me paternally on the arm. His face had broken into a most unexpected smile. "Yes," he said, "Mr. Dobrynin came in here often. And he would sit right there — exactly where your husband is sitting."

By the time I'd finished gushing about that, Clifton's smile had faded.

"Oh, that poor young man!" he said sadly. "What a terrible, tragic way for him to die."

Then, as if to extricate himself from a memory just too painful, he turned away and walked to a shelf, where he busied himself rearranging bottles.

I kicked Tony's leg, signaling that we were in luck. I saw him nod in affirmation.

The old bartender stole a quick glance at us over his shoulder, as if he were conflicted, as if he wouldn't mind speaking more about Peter Dobrynin but thought it might be indiscreet.

Noting the glance, I pressed on, talking a mile a minute about all the scandalous things I used to read in the New York papers I'd had delivered to my Spokane home.

Finally, he broke. "I want you to know

that he was not what they said about him in the papers! Mr. Dobrynin was a kind gentleman — generous and very polite. Oh yes, there was many a night when he drank much more than he should have, but he never misbehaved in this establishment. That talk of his being ejected from our bar is all nonsense. That never happened here. Never."

He waited for a response from me, as if I might find his defense of Dobrynin impossible to believe. I said nothing.

There was nothing that could dam the flood of the bartender's memories now. They broke the dike and rushed relentlessly on. As he reminisced, he needlessly wiped the top of the bar and tidied up.

"Certainly he did some . . . *unusual* things here. But they were never harmful to anyone. He was an artist, Mr. Dobrynin, an eccentric. And quite an artist he was, as I'm sure I needn't tell you. Why, he once gave me tickets to see him perform. I took my young niece. How thrilling that was! He was grand."

"What do you mean when you say he was an eccentric?"

He smiled indulgently. "Well, he would often come in with pets . . . animals. Now, of course pets are not allowed in eating establishments in this country. But once, I remember he was with another dancer, a gentleman from the Netherlands, I believe, and Mr. Dobrynin had a parrot on his shoulder. And the parrot was wearing the same clothing as Mr. Dobrynin — the same hat, the same jacket. The bird spoke only in Dutch, and Mr. Dobrynin assured me that while its language was foul, no one would understand it.

"Oh, yes indeed. And once he brought in a wonderful labrador retriever he said he'd found in the street. He'd bought it a muffler, and he sat right here feeding it steak tartare. Oh, yes indeed, he was fond of animals — and he always dressed them."

The man wheeled suddenly and opened a glass cabinet, removing a lovely bottle. He held it up. "Delamain," he said fondly. "The brandy Mr. Dobrynin loved. How often he would insist I have a drink with him . . . like this." He reached for a snifter, placed it on the bar, poured out a little of the pale brown liquid, and downed it in one gulp. Then he filled the glass with water, drank that, gargled daintily, and spat the water out. It was both fastidious and remarkably vulgar. This prissy bartender was really something.

He looked at me slyly, as if his mind were

on some private joke. Then he moved close and began to speak in a conspiratorial voice. "To tell the entire truth," he said, "I did once have to ask Mr. Dobrynin to leave. Just once." He shook his head a little sadly. "He came in quite late one evening, sat in his usual spot. He had a friend with him. A cat. A big fluffy cat with a charming ruff on its chest. He was quite in his cups that night. He had put one of those ballet costumes that the ladies wear on the little beast."

"A tutu?" I inquired anxiously.

"Yes. A skirt. It was very amusing. Not that the kitty seemed to mind. It just stayed on top of the bar while he drank. But as I said, Mr. Dobrynin was over the limit that night. He started taking the cat around to all the tables, introducing it to everyone, and several of the customers objected. When the manager told him he would have to desist, he became quite angry. He did have a temper, you know. He claimed we'd insulted the cat. Made a horrible fuss before he finally left. Yes, he said we'd insulted a great dancer, Anna Pavlova."

Tony looked over at me, and I know I looked like a ghost. My heart was pounding. What I had been looking for, I'd found — that single, overwhelmingly absurd fact . . . a cat in a tutu . . . on the bar . . . the thing that made this whole incredible mystery comprehensible. But it was a repellent revelation. I knew now who had murdered Peter Dobrynin. And why. And that knowledge made me sick.

"I think you mean Anna Pavlova *Smith*," Tony corrected the old man.

"Oh, yes. Of course. That was the name. My goodness, what loyal fans you must be, to know a thing so small as that! He would have been very happy — God rest his soul — to know both of you."

I knew that if I started to laugh I would start to cry. And that if I started to cry, I would never stop. Tony helped me out into the bracing evening air.

24

I had to be especially careful in laying this, the final trap. No one under heaven would believe my story unless the proof was incontestable.

I gave Basillio no details, but he agreed to help anyway. I don't think he even wanted to know *what* I was planning — as it was, even the name "Peter Dobrynin" was getting to be too much for him.

The ad I placed in the Sunday *New York Times* was short and to the point:

CAT FOUND. ANNA PAVLOVA SMITH READY TO RETURN HOME. FEE REQUIRED. CALL 212-653-6228 AFTER SIX P.M.

I moved in to Tony's hotel room on Saturday afternoon. The phone number in the ad was in fact that of his hotel room. And if my suspicion proved correct, the person to whom the ad was directed would read it Saturday night, when the *Times* hit the stands.

Tony was happy to have me as a guest, but he was puzzled as to why I had brought Bushy along with me in his carrier.

"We need all the help we can get," I said cryptically, setting Bushy free and watching him inspect the room tentatively. He didn't much like it.

"Do I need a gun for this one, Swede?" Tony asked, no doubt making fun of my secretive behavior.

"No. All you need to do is listen and follow instructions."

He sat down primly on the bed. "I'm all ears."

"You'll get a phone call tonight. If not tonight, never. Someone will ask what the fee is for Anna Pavlova Smith. You'll tell the caller the price is five thousand dollars. Say you'll take a check. If it is a check it must be made out to cash, dated Monday, and endorsed on the back. The caller must come to your hotel room immediately. Have you got that?"

"Yeah. Fine. But then what happens when they get here?"

"Take the money and hand over Anna Pavlova Smith."

He found that funny. "And where do I find Miss Smith?"

I pointed at Bushy.

"You mean you want me to give away your cat!"

"Just follow instructions, Tony, and

everthing will be fine."

"How about calling old man Brodsky? He might get a kick out of the fact that his crack investigator is blowing what's left of the expense account. I mean, that guy could *use* a laugh."

I sat down on the one easy chair and began the vigil. I had brought along a book — *Madame Bovary*, in an old paperback edition, which I tend to reread every three or four years. The bookmark was set at page sixty-two. Emma and Charles were riding in their carriage.

"What's the matter with you?" Tony asked suddenly.

"Nothing," I replied.

"You're acting strange. You're too cool. Like you were waiting for a delivery of cat food, not a murderer."

"What would you have me do, Tony? Jump around? Tremble?"

"Do something other than just sit there reading!"

He was right. I *was* strangely calm. No, not calm, sad. If what I thought would happen did happen, then I would be *truly* sad.

"Besides, how do you know this person is going to see the ad? It seems like a one-in-a-million shot," Tony observed.

"Believe me, the murderer will see the ad. The murderer is looking for such an ad, always looking. Don't you understand?"

"How many times have I heard that awful phrase tumble from your bee-stung lips, I wonder?" Tony grinned and busied himself by trying to amuse Bushy. The hours went by. At ten that evening, Tony said: "You think we may have a problem?"

"Be patient, Tony. Soon. It'll happen soon."

"I think maybe you don't know what you're doing here. Everybody makes mistakes, Swede."

I turned on him in a fury. "What do you want, the ghost of Peter Dobrynin dancing across the room? Or do you want me shivering in a corner, waiting for the killer, knowing that my life and yours are at risk? Or maybe you want the police here backing me up! Just what *do* you want?"

"Calm down, will you? I was just pulling your leg a little!"

The phone rang. I held Tony back until the third ring. I closed *Madame Bovary* and told him, "Pick it up now, Tony. Remember, say exactly what I told you to."

Tony answered the phone, following my instructions to the letter. When he hung up, he looked pale.

"Damn," he said hoarsely. "You were right. She's on her way over right now. With the money. Who would ever figure it. Five grand — for what? A nonexistent cat? Who *is* this cat?"

"Did you recognize the voice, Tony?"

"No. She had an accent. I never believed in a million years we would get any kind of call. Never."

"You ought to trust your Aunt Alice," I said, with no small touch of malice.

"Now what?" he asked. For the first time, he appeared to be a bit frightened. My observation made me realize that I, too, and also for the first time, was a bit frightened.

I picked up the unhappy Bushy and deposited him once more in the carrier. Then I placed the carrier on the bed.

"Okay, Tony. Here's the next part of the plan. When your visitor enters, just show her the carrier. Say you've got A.P.S. inside there. Do *not* open the box until you've got the money in your hands. If it's cash, count it. If it's a check, make sure it's made out the way I said. I'm going to be waiting in the bathroom. Understand all that?"

"Yes. Then what do I do?"

"Don't worry about that. It'll all work out."

I walked into the bathroom and turned off

the light. I left the door open just a crack. It was chilly in there.

My eyes were growing accustomed to the darkness; I could see the shiny white shower curtain. It was drawn across the tub as though someone were in there showering. I felt the urge to take a peek, but of course I knew no one was there.

The darkness and the waiting began to oppress me. I had the strangest sense that I was about to go onstage. It was the old actor's nightmare: walking onstage totally unprepared . . . no idea what the play is . . . what your role is . . . who the other players are . . . no memory . . . struck dumb.

"Come in."

It was Tony's voice. I almost panicked. Why hadn't I heard the knock on the door? Perhaps it had been too soft. But that had been Tony's voice. I pressed my ear up to the slit of space between the door and the jamb. I heard movement in the outer room. I heard a voice that didn't belong to Tony. I heard the words "Anna Pavlova Smith."

Then I heard Basillio say distinctly, "Before we go any further, let me see the money."

No sound. Then a burst of activity. Mumbled words. A shuffle of feet. I heard the rustle of paper. Was money being exchanged? Counted? I heard Tony's footfalls heading over to the floor lamp. Maybe he was inspecting the check.

It was time for me to show myself. I had waited this long only because it was important for the money to have changed hands.

I strode out of the dark room and shut — no, slammed — the door behind me.

A small, handsome black woman stood near the bed. She stared at me with horrified eyes. "Why are *you* here?" she asked, but instead of waiting for an answer she ran for the door.

"Tony!" I screamed out.

He lurched toward the door, slamming into it and sending our visitor reeling to one side.

"Please," I said, "just stay where you are! No one is going to hurt you!"

The woman was breathing hard, but she remained still.

I turned to Tony, who was waving the check at me. "I don't think we were all properly introduced the last time," I said, looking first at him and then at the woman. "Tony, do you remember Lucia Maury's nurse?"

I walked to the bed and, as the saying goes, let the cat out of the bag. "This isn't the one you were sent to fetch," I said to the woman. Then I sat down on the bed, suddenly exhausted.

Tony sat beside me, the check still in his hand. "Are you ready to tell me what's happening now?"

"It's already happened," I said wearily. "We're just doing the cleaning up. Making sure everyone pays his own piper.

"You see, a number of years ago, Lucia Maury fell in love with a great dancer. She knew she was just one in a long line of his lovers, but to her that didn't matter. She loved him very much. In fact, the only thing she loved as much was her cat, a Maine coon named Splat.

"The dancer had a major drinking problem. And one of his eccentricities was to take animals and dress them outlandishly, then take them along with him on his drinking sprees. He thought it was cute. While he was carrying on the affair with Lucia, her cat became one of his companions. For some crazy reason of his own, he decided to call the cat "Anna Pavlova Smith" — even though Splat was a male. Lucia begged him not to take the cat out of her apartment, but he did it anyway. He did it and he kept doing it, maybe even without her knowledge sometimes. Then, the worst possible thing happened. On one of his pub crawls, he lost sight of Anna Pavlova Smith. The cat wandered off and entered the world of the lost and lonely. Lucia searched the streets, posted notices, offered rewards for the return of the cat. Dobrynin searched the shelters. But no, poor Splat was gone. And Lucia rightly blamed the dancer.

"She broke off the affair. And she told everyone that Splat had died from an illness. But she never believed he was dead. She continued to look for him. Years passed. Her hatred of Dobrynin grew. After he became a derelict — after, presumably, he'd had a series of breakdowns — he started contacting her again. This only reinforced her hatred of him, and soon that hatred became all-consuming.

"As for Dobrynin, by then calling himself 'Lenny,' he still recognized his guilt — even in his psychosis. And eventually his guilt became a part of the psychosis. He kept searching for the cat. He began to feed strays all over the city, hoping that Anna Pavlova Smith might be among them. For him, the missing cat had become an obsession. As his madness grew, the cat grew into a delusional monster who would someday pay him back for his crime.

"In fact, though, it was Lucia who paid him back . . . who lured him to Lincoln

Center and shot him there on that balcony. And then, in an act of utter contempt for his art, for his dancing feet, removed his shoes and left him there to die barefoot, unprotected, as he had allowed Splat to vanish into the cold city.

"And then there was one final act of vengeance. She paid someone — very likely one of the homeless people who camp around Lincoln Center — to paint the name on the hearse that would carry Peter Dobrynin to his grave. As if Dobrynin would know the reason for his own funeral. There is no doubt in my mind that Lucia Maury is as mad as her lover ever was."

"But what about Basil?" Tony interjected. "In his confession he said that Vol Teak planned the murder."

"No, Tony. Not exactly. He said he knew nothing about the murder itself — only that Vol Teak had paid him to bring Lenny to the theater. But the point is, given the things Frank Brodsky had threatened him with, Basil would have said anything. He told us what we wanted to hear."

By this time, the nurse had taken a seat and was listening to the wrap-up as closely as Tony was. He got up and poured water for each of us.

"When did you figure all this out? How

long have you been sitting on it?"

"Not that long. It gathered its own momentum. But it was that nightmarish sketch of the cat made by Dobrynin that helped me put it all together — the specter of a monster cat tracking him, the feeding of the stray cats with Russian food, his bare feet."

"I saw the cat picture in the hospital too," Tony said. "I didn't notice anything special about it, other than its complete craziness."

"Neither did I, at first. But then I realized that Dobrynin had drawn his rendition of a Maine coon cat. And Lucia's Splat was such a breed — the same as Bushy."

Tony looked over at the silent nurse, who visibly tensed when he asked, "What are we going to do about . . . her?"

I sighed heavily. "I'm really sorry," I said, addressing the nurse directly, "but we're going to need you, when we take the check to the detective who arrested Lucia in the first place." I turned back to Tony. "The one who was forced to release her, thanks to our brilliant work."

"So much for genius," he said.

Bushy was rubbing himself against the nurse's legs, soliciting admiration. But he didn't get any — the nurse seemed to have drifted off to some faraway place.

25

It was one o'clock in the morning when Tony, the Haitian nurse (Madeline, by name), and I showed up unannounced on the doorstep of Frank Brodsky.

I had originally planned to contact the police directly, but I realized that I owed my employer an explanation first, at the very least. And I entertained the hope that I could leave it to him to make the presentation to the police, to tie all the loose ends together.

He greeted us in his bathrobe. Clearly we had roused him from sleep, but he was ever the gentleman, leading us all up the stairs to his small, elegant conference room. He apologized that he could offer us no coffee, but he went to great effort to provide us with water in glasses of sparkling crystal.

Tony, Madeline, and I sat down at the table. Frank Brodsky remained standing.

I began to tell my story in detail, culminating with the trap which had caught Madeline and which, with all other evidence, circumstantial and otherwise, clearly revealed that Lucia Maury had indeed murdered Peter Dobrynin.

The lawyer didn't interrupt once. From time to time he circled the table, but he never sat and he never spoke.

By the time I'd finished my recitation it was a little after two in the morning. I drank some water and waited.

For the longest time Brodsky didn't respond to what I had said. He inspected one of his paintings, then some scuff marks on a table leg, then a small mark on the ceiling. Finally he sat down wearily in his usual chair at the head of the long, lovely table.

"You look very tired, Miss Nestleton," he said.

"It has been a long night," I admitted.

He looked at Tony and Madeline. "You *all* look tired," he said.

Again there was that silence; only this time it was making me distinctly uncomfortable. Why hadn't he congratulated me? Where was his joy at hearing that this ugly murder had finally been solved? Where, in fact, was his appreciation for what I had accomplished?

He smiled at me broadly, kindly, as if my fatigue were causing him real concern.

"I have a very good idea," he said. He paused. "Do you want to hear my idea?"

"Of course," I answered. But then he looked at Tony and Madeline. He wanted them to hear his idea also. They made no response, which was enough for him.

"I think," he said, "that you should stay here a little while and rest up. There is room for all of you to take a nap. Then you should all take a cab home at my expense, have a good meal at my expense, and go to sleep. In the morning, when you wake up, you should have some fresh orange juice. And then just forget everything you've told me this evening."

I stared at him dumbly. Was he joking? Was this his idea of a folksy joke? Then I realized that he was quite serious. I looked at Tony. He looked at me, perplexed. I looked at Madeline. Her eyes were fixed on a painting hung high on a wall.

My response to his suggestion was nakedly venomous: "Didn't you hear what I just told you, Mr. Brodsky? Weren't you listening? Perhaps I can recite the whole story again when you're fully awake."

He smiled. "Ah, Miss Nestleton, I heard every word you said. Every word. I paid close attention. But I see you are not going to take me up on my suggestion. I see you are here, in a sense, demanding some kind of action."

He shook his head from side to side, slowly and sadly.

"Doesn't it strike you as strange, Miss Nestleton, that the same woman I hired as a criminal investigator to clear Lucia Maury's name has ended up dirtying it? As bizarre, Miss Nestleton, that you were hired to help *defend* Lucia Maury but seem to have spent all your time and energy — *considerable* energy, I might add — trying to *convict* Lucia Maury?"

"What precisely are you saying, Mr. Brodsky?"

"Nothing very profound. It just seems to me that you are engaged in an odd form of betrayal."

"Betrayal? How dare you accuse me of that! Lucia Maury is my friend, but I hired on to conduct an objective investigation!"

My fury subsided as quickly as it had erupted. In its place came a deadening realization: The lawyer was absolutely right. I was handing Lucia over to the hangman. It just hadn't dawned on me to characterize this as "betrayal." I had simply followed one lead after another. I had sought the truth. I had pursued a murderer. Yet, when all was said and done, I would have to accuse Lucia Maury. But there was no other way!

"Perhaps," I finally said to him, "the difference between you and me is that I can't be bought, intellectually." It was a cruel thing to say, and a flash of hatred and anger creased his usually cherubic face. Then he smiled, inclined his head as if I had scored a point, and folded his hands in front of him.

"Well, Miss Nestleton, we shouldn't get into personalities. So let us get back to reason. You come here at one in the morning with an outlandish, unproven, un-substantiated tale about my client, and you expect me to do something about it. This tale you told me contradicts a signed con-fession, freely given, which clearly names Vol Teak as the individual who shot and killed Peter Dobrynin. May I remind you that Vol Teak had a rational motive for murder: blackmail. According to the police and the district attorney, this case is closed. According to all rules of evidence and pro-cedure, this case is closed. According to all logic, this case is closed."

Then Tony said: "That confession was coerced."

"You mean I *beat* Basil?" Mr. Brodsky asked, sarcastically.

"You did worse than that! Basil is a fright-ened, borderline, strung-out street addict. I don't think he had any idea what his life was twenty-four hours earlier. You planted the diamonds on him, said they were from a beaten diamond dealer, and he was crazed enough to believe that he did it. Hell, for people like Basil it doesn't matter if they really committed a crime; if the police believe they did it, then they did it! You hustled him, Mr. Brodsky. You abused him! You terrorized the poor bastard. So he told you what you wanted to hear. And none of us complained, because we thought we knew that Vol Teak was guilty. But now we know something else. And the case against Vol Teak is airtight only for as long as Basil's phony confession holds up. Which may be only another five minutes!"

Tony paused, angry, his voice breaking. It was obvious that Basil's confession and the lawyer's part in it had been rankling for a long time.

Frank Brodsky didn't respond. He poured himself a few sips of water, then looked around expansively. He said something in French to Madeline, who just nodded. It dawned on me that for all I knew it might have been Frank Brodsky who had originally obtained the Haitian nurse for Lucia.

"I think, Miss Nestleton," he finally said, pushing the water glass along the table as if it were a child's toy, "I am going to have to reveal some confidences you have shared with me." I had no idea what he could mean.

"My past isn't so mysterious, though I'd like to think it is," I replied good-humoredly, seeing as he seemed ready to reveal some desperate act I'd once committed.

But he didn't smile. He said: "You once told me, Miss Nestleton, that you are friendly with a Detective Rothwax of the NYPD. I believe you also told me that you both worked together some time back in a special investigative unit, called RETRO, I believe."

"Well," I replied gingerly, not sure where this was heading, "that's true."

He smiled. "I hope you won't be angry with me, Miss Nestleton, but I took the liberty some time ago of contacting this detective, although he wasn't easy to find. I just wanted his evaluation of you. After all, Miss Nestleton, since I was spending money to hire you, I thought it wise to get an outside evaluation. In other words, when you introduced me to him just before Basil confessed, we had already met secretly."

He looked around at all of us before he proceeded.

"Detective Rothwax shared with me his

nickname for you: 'Cat Woman.' Naturally, when I heard this I was curious as to the origin of such a strange name for so beautiful and intelligent a woman as yourself, Miss Nestleton."

He seemed to wait for affirmation from the assembled that I was, indeed, beautiful and intelligent. Then he continued.

"Detective Rothwax explained that while you were a crackerjack investigator — yes, I remember that he did use that charming old-fashioned word, 'crackerjack' — you were obsessed with things feline. To such an extent, Detective Rothwax said, that once in a while you enter a fantasy world that has nothing at all to do with real crimes committed by real people in the real world."

I stood up in a rage. My body was trembling. I literally shouted at the lawyer: "Obsession? Fantasy? Real?"

I looked at Tony. "Give me that check!" He reached into his pocket, pulled out the folded check, and handed it to me.

Holding the check out in front of Brodsky so that he could clearly see it, I shouted: "Is this a fantasy? Is this an obsession? Look at it, Mr. Brodsky! Look at it! It is made out to cash! It is signed by Lucia Maury! It is in payment for the return of a Maine coon cat called 'Anna Pavlova Smith,' better known as 'Splat'! And Lucia gave this check to Madeline last night to deliver to a hotel room, because an ad had been placed in the paper saying that someone had found Anna Pavlova Smith — the cat that a drunk Peter Dobrynin took barhopping and lost! The cat whose loss Lucia Maury eventually avenged by putting a bullet hole in the dancer's forehead on Christmas Eve, after she had given him a ticket to *The Nutcracker*!"

"Calm down, Miss Nestleton! You must calm down!"

"No! I'm *not* going to calm down! I'm just going to get out of here! But let me give you a small assignment, counselor, in order to check my fantasy level. Just call up your client and ask her for a letter from her vet certifying that her cat Splat was 'put down' as she has always claimed . . . or the cremation certificate. See if she can corroborate her story that poor Splat died of natural causes three years ago. You do that, Mr. Brodsky, and also, while you're having that discussion, ask her about this check."

I motioned to Tony. He stood up and we both walked to the door. I turned to Madeline. "Send my best to Lucia. Tell her that I'm sorry I had to raise her hopes about Splat by advertising that he was found. Tell her there was no other way for me to flush her out. And also tell her, Madeline, that the odds of a house cat surviving abandonment on the city streets are greater than the distance between earth and the outer limits of the expanding universe to one."

Tony and I walked out of the room and started down the flight of stairs.

"Wait! Please, Miss Nestleton, wait!" I turned and saw Frank Brodsky standing at the top of the stairs. He seemed extremely agitated, and I was suddenly ashamed that I had screamed at him. After all, he was an old man.

I waited with Tony. Brodsky started to climb down a few steps, to get closer to me, then thought the better of it and stayed at the top of the landing, catching his breath and holding on to the staircase.

"Please listen to me just for a moment! I am sorry I insulted you! It was not my intention! Hear me out, please!"

I could see the sweat on his forehead and along his upper lip.

"It will take but a moment! And then you can leave; yes, then you can do whatever you want!" He began to breathe more evenly. "Suppose, Miss Nestleton, that what you have told me is true. This would mean that Lucia Maury is a very disturbed woman, a woman who should be in a mental hospital for treatment. Only a madwoman would murder a man because he innocently lost her cat while it was in his drunken care. We can all agree on that, can't we, Miss Nestleton?

"Yet, as you well know, it is virtually impossible now to prove insanity to a sitting jury. And that means that Lucia Maury might well spend the next twenty years in prison. Oh, Miss Nestleton, no matter how deranged she may be, she does not deserve that! Who knows what else Peter Dobrynin did to her? You yourself told me that he routinely tormented and degraded women. No doubt he did the same to Lucia. No doubt he drove her to that insane act." He wiped the sweat off his brow with the sleeve of his bathrobe. I waited for him to speak again, to continue, but he just stood there, staring at me imploringly.

"I don't understand you," I finally said. "I'm not sure what you're telling me. What do you want me to do?"

"Do nothing, Miss Nestleton," he replied.

"Nothing."

"Yes, Miss Nestleton, nothing. I will go to the District Attorney and inform him of how Basil was coerced into his confession.

That will clear Vol Teak of the murder charge, though not of the charges that he extorted money from ballet companies."

"And then what, Mr. Brodsky?"

"Nothing. Let it become one of the thousands of unsolved crimes. As for Lucia Maury, I will see to it that she is committed to a psychiatric hospital in her native Delaware."

I turned and started down the steps again. Just as Tony and I were walking through the front door I heard him plead: "Think about it! Think about everything! Think of Lucia!"

Once outside, we walked slowly down the deserted street, leaning into the cold wind. "What are you going to do?" Tony asked, holding my arm tightly.

"I don't know, but I want to be alone for a while."

26

The buzzer kept ringing. Whoever it was wouldn't stop. I went into my bedroom and shut the door and buried my head in a pillow. But still I could hear it. Finally, exasperated, I buzzed the intruder in.

Of course it was Tony. "What the hell is the matter with you, Swede? I've been calling you for two days! Why don't you answer the phone or return messages?"

"Nothing to say."

He came inside and started to prowl about. Pancho glared at him. Bushy ignored him. I made him a cup of instant coffee.

"Well, have you made a decision yet?" he asked.

"About what?"

"About whether you're going to Paris in the spring. You know damn well what I'm talking about!"

"I've done nothing," I admitted.

"It sure is, as they say, a tough nut to crack," he noted, gulping down what was left of the coffee and then picking Bushy up in his arms and threatening, by means of panto-mime, to fling him through the window.

Then he gently dropped Bushy onto the sofa, telling my poor beautiful cat: "You'd last about three minutes as a stray, Bushy. You're a decadent cat."

It's odd how a silly little conversation can have a greater impact on a listener than a profound one. Particularly words said to a cat. I mean, for almost forty-eight hours before Tony told Bushy he wouldn't last three minutes as a stray, I was in a very bad state. I didn't know what to do. I couldn't decide where my responsibilities lay. To call the police? To forget the police? To allow Lucia to escape the consequences of her actions? And I had also brooded over the facts of the case. Had I interpreted them correctly? Was any part of my analysis fantasy rather than fact? Had I caught the wrong person with the wrong bait? Was there any other conceivable motive for Lucia to have written and sent that check?

On and on it had gone, with no light visible at the end of the tunnel. I could make no decision. I could find no finality. I couldn't finish the role or the script.

And then Tony had spoken those silly words, and his mentioning the word "stray" had reminded me of those poor stray cats in Riverside Park that had not eaten a good Russian meal, or perhaps any meal at all, since Dobrynin died.

Right there, right then, I decided to feed them. Oh, I know it was stupid. It was an obvious attempt to postpone serious activity, a handy excuse for not dealing with the real problem at hand — but I wanted to do it. I suddenly *had* to do it. It became my immediate responsibility.

I threw on my muffler, coat, and sweater. Tony had yet to shed his outer garments, so I just pulled him out of the apartment along with me.

"What's the matter with you, Swede? What's going on?"

"We're going to feed some cats, Tony."

"What cats?"

"The ones Dobrynin used to feed. The ones in Riverside Park, Tony. It's time you and I did some good deeds."

"I don't have enough cash for The Russian Tea Room."

"We have another option."

The cab took us to Eighth Avenue in the fifties. I remembered a Russian takeout kitchen just west of Eighth Avenue, across the street from a post office.

It was close to four in the afternoon, and cold. We moved in and out of the side streets until we found the place, nestling in a gloomy storefront, its windows all but pa-

274

pered over with dozens of rave reviews from the local food critics, including a splendid one from *The Village Voice.*

Inside was a small, skinny, brooding man with an enormous checked apron. He had long sideburns and a flattened nose.

"I'd like some blini with sour cream and caviar, an order of chicken Kiev, and a dozen pirogi."

He didn't say a word after I'd ordered, just pointed a finger. I turned toward what he'd pointed at — freezers along the wall. Tony laughed. The place had what we wanted, but all of it was frozen.

"Do you have a microwave?" I asked.

"Of course," he replied.

Five minutes later we were half walking, half trotting uptown toward Riverside Park.

Tony kept muttering. "This is the stupidest thing I ever let you rope me into, Swede. Do you know how crazy this is? Two people past forty, racing uptown with heated Russian food to feed alley cats in Riverside Park!"

"They're not alley cats, Tony," I cautioned.

We entered the park at Seventy-second Street, racing against the lengthening shadows: We wouldn't have dreamed of entering that or any other city park after nightfall.

"What was that woman's name?" I asked as we approached the boat basin.

"What woman?"

"The homeless woman with the shopping cart. The one who showed us the cats. The one who used to get the food for Dobrynin."

"I don't remember."

It didn't matter, because she wasn't there. The walkway along the boat basin was devoid of homeless people, empty of all people except the ever-present joggers, muffled against the cold wind but plodding on.

"The cats were up there," Tony said, pointing east. We walked away from the water up the path.

"There's the iron railing!" I called out, like an excited and happy child. I was carrying the pirogi. Tony was carrying the blini, the small containers of sour cream and caviar, and the chicken Kiev.

I started to laugh out loud.

"What's the matter with you, Swede?"

"It's just making me giddy, thinking of all those lovely cats digging into the blini with caviar and sour cream. If I was a cat I would love any kind of crepes — and blini with caviar . . . my God!"

We reached the railing. "Get sticks, Tony. Get some sticks." He found us some branches, and even a broken sponge-mop stick with the metal hinge still attached.

Like two mad people we ran the implements raucously along the iron railings, setting up a terrible racket. The cats' dinner bell had sounded.

We waited. Nothing. No movement at all. I stared at the rock outcroppings and brush on the other side of the railing   the spot from which the cats had emerged the last time we were there.

Nothing. No movement. No cats. And it was getting darker.

The giddiness had vanished. I grabbed Tony's arm desperately. "Where *are* they?" I cried out. "Why won't they come?"

"Let's leave the food and get out of here," Tony said. He shook my arm off, knelt down and opened the packages, and slipped the food through the fence onto the ground. I bent down to hand him my parcel of pirogi, and he opened it and pushed it through the railing.

"Let's go," he said, straightening up to take hold of my arm again and lead me out of the park.

That's when I saw the two points of light, deep in the brush.

"Wait, Tony! Wait!"

Then the two points of light vanished. But

they *had* been cat's eyes. I knew it.

I stared hard into the growing darkness. Something was moving. Yes, a shape moving . . . It was a cat. A large, strong, dark cat. A smokey-blue cat with a chest ruff. A Maine coon.

"Tony, look there! Look there!" I picked up one of the sticks and began to bang it against the railing, harder and harder.

"Where Swede? Where? I don't see anything!"

"It's Splat, Tony! It's Anna Pavlova Smith! He's alive!"

I dropped the stick, exhausted, waiting. Silence. I stared. What had happened? The cat had vanished. It was gone. But I *knew* I had seen him . . . or one like him.

"Please!" Tony said imploringly, placing his arm gently around my neck. "Please, let's go. They'll find the food."

We walked slowly out of the park. A terrible sadness descended upon me. It made my limbs weak and my step unsteady.

Tony took me to a bar on Broadway. He ordered two bottles of ale.

"Are you okay now?" he asked.

I nodded, then poured some of the ale from the bottle into the glass. It was warm and quiet in the bar. I didn't drink.

"What did you *really* see there?" he asked.

"Now, I'm not sure."

"It couldn't have been Lucia's cat. There's no chance he survived three years on the city streets. At best, somebody took him in."

I didn't reply. I sipped some of the ale. It was nutty and sweet.

"And besides, Swede, you know what your grandmother says."

I burst out laughing in spite of myself. "But Tony, you told me that if you ever heard another line from *The Wit and Wisdom of Grandma Nestleton*, you were going to jump off the Chrysler Building."

Tony squirmed. "Well, Swede, since you've been reduced to seeing visions in parks, maybe one of her gems would help you to . . . you know . . . ease back into reality. That's what old ladies on frigid Minnesota dairy farms are all about — reality. Hard, cold, unvarnished, wood-chopping reality."

"Okay, Tony, I'll bite. Which gem?"

"Oh, come on, you know the one, Swede! Your grandmother used to say: 'it's okay to die for a cat — but not to kill for one.' "

"She never said that, Tony!"

"Well, maybe one of her friends said it. Or the farm-implements dealer."

"And maybe I saw Anna Pavlova Smith," I replied bitterly.

We were silent. I drank some more ale. It was a tad too cold for my taste.

"Do you have any change, Tony?" I asked.

"What for?"

"It's time I made a telephone call." He leaned over and kissed me on the lips, then reached down into his right-hand pocket and produced a quarter.

I looked around and saw a pay phone on the wall, near the rest rooms. I walked toward it, holding the quarter gingerly between two fingers.

I remembered the phrase they always use in gangster movies: "drop a dime."

That's exactly what I was going to do: Call the police. "Drop a dime" — a quarter, after inflation — on my friend Lucia Maury. She was a murderer. She had to be accused and charged with the crime. If she had been psychotic at the moment she pulled the trigger, that would be up to a jury to decide.

Cats? Dancers? Passions? All that, I could at last see clearly, was beside the point. A human being had been murdered. As soon as I reached the phone I "dropped the dime" — quarter. But unlike the informers in all those gangster movies, I felt no glee whatsoever.